THE IMPATIENT LORD

DRAGON LORDS: A QURILIXEN WORLD NOVEL

MICHELLE M. PILLOW

MICHELLE M. PILLOW® - MICHELLEPILLOW.COM

Third Edition Printing July 2018

Second Edition Printing April 2015

First Edition Printing March 2014

Published by The Raven Books LLC

ISBN 13: 978-1-62501-176-3

ABOUT THE IMPATIENT LORD

DRAGON LORDS 8

Dragon-shifter Romance

by Michelle M. Pillow

An unlucky bride...

Riona Grey lives life on her own terms, traveling wherever the next spaceship is flying and doing what she must in order to get by. When her luck turns sour, she finds herself on a bridal ship heading to a marriage ceremony. A planet full of dragon-shifters seeking mates wasn't exactly what she had in mind as a final destination. Just when she thinks things couldn't possibly get worse, she wakes up months later in an isolation chamber with a sexy, hovering dragon-shifter by her side telling her they're meant to be together…forever.

The impatient groom...

After years of failed marriage attempts at the Breeding Festivals, the gods finally revealed Lord Mirek's bride…a day too late. Eager to have her, he defied tradition and laid claim. But it is a mistake to go against the gods and his new wife was the one to pay the price of his impatience.

Now almost a year later, his bride is finally waking from her deep sleep. With one look from her, he feels the eagerness to claim her overtaking him once more. Fearful she'll slip through his grasp once again, he's hesitant to anger the gods by taking her to his bed too soon. But, how can he resist the one thing that would make his life complete, especially when she looks at him with eyes of a seductress? This is one test he can't fail, and yet with one of her sweet kisses he knows he may already have lost.

NEW TO DRAGON LORDS?

Dragon Lords books 1-8 follow a concurrent time line. The fun of this is that the events you read in one book might be examined from a different point of view, sometimes with overlapping or expanded scenes, sometimes with events you might have wondered about in another book. You might even discover secrets as characters interact with each other. I recommend reading them in order to get the full effect. However if you bought the books out of order, no worries, each book is technically a standalone story for the hero and heroine.

DRAGON LORDS SERIES

PART OF THE QURILIXEN WORLD COLLECTION

Dragon Lords Books 1 - 4

The dragon-shifting princes have no problem with commitment. In one night, they will meet and choose their life mate in a simplistic ceremony involving the removing of masks and the crushing of crystals. With very few words spoken and the shortest, most bizarre courtship in history, they will bond to their women forever. And once bonded, these men don't let go...

Too bad nobody explained this to their brides.

Dragon Lords Books 5-8

The noblemen brothers aren't new to the

sacred Qurilixian bridal ceremony. After several failed attempts at finding a bride, it's hard to get excited about yet another festival. No matter how honorable they try to live, it would seem fate thinks them unworthy of such happiness—that is until now.

With very few words spoken and the shortest, most bizarre courtship in history, they will bond to their women forever. And once bonded, these men don't let go...

Too bad nobody explained this to their brides.

Dragon Lords Book 9

Before four princes and four noblemen found their brides, before the death of the Var King Attor and the threat of the Tyoe miners, there was a time of peace on the planet of Qurilixen. It was not a strong peace, but it had lasted for quite some time between the cat-shifting Var kingdom and their northern neighbors the dragon-shifting Draig. It lasted because both sides had very little to do with each other.

This was the time before the great war came to rift the planet apart—dragon against cat. The only battles were skirmishes along the borderlands over territory and drunken brawls that erupted to prove which shifter side was of superior strength. It is here the dragons found their queen.

Spin-off Series

Dragon Lords is the first installment in the multiple bestselling romance series. As of this publication, there are nine Dragon Lords books.

The series continues with the *Lords of the Var*® series, Space Lords series, Dynasty Lords Series, Captured by a Dragon-Shifter series, Galaxy Alien Mail Order Brides series, and Qurilixen Lords series.

There will be more books and more series to come. They can be read alone, but the author recommends reading books in order of release.

For details please visit www.michellepillow.com

WELCOME TO QURILIXEN

QURILIXEN WORLD NOVELS

Dragon Lords Series

Barbarian Prince

Perfect Prince

Dark Prince

Warrior Prince

His Highness The Duke

The Stubborn Lord

The Reluctant Lord

The Impatient Lord

The Dragon's Queen

***Lords of the Var*® Series**

The Savage King

The Playful Prince

The Bound Prince

The Rogue Prince

The Pirate Prince

Captured by a Dragon-Shifter Series

Determined Prince

Rebellious Prince

Stranded with the Cajun

Hunted by the Dragon

Mischievous Prince

Headstrong Prince

Space Lords Series

His Frost Maiden

His Fire Maiden

His Metal Maiden

His Earth Maiden

His Woodland Maiden

Dynasty Lords Series

Seduction of the Phoenix
Temptation of the Butterfly

To learn more about the Qurilixen World series of books and to stay up to date on the latest book list visit www.MichellePillow.com

AUTHOR UPDATES

To stay informed about when a new book in the series installments is released, sign up for updates:

michellepillow.com/author-updates

ACKNOWLEDGMENTS

TO MY READERS & PILLOW FIGHTERS:

Writing can be a solitary career. Authors spend hours upon hours at a computer, staring at a screen, talking to imaginary friends and playing Goddess of Thier Universe. Hey, I'm not complaining. I get to make things up for a living. I love my job and without you, the readers, I wouldn't have a job. So, to the readers—Thank You. Not only do you read the books, you send me emails, leave reviews, help entertain those solitary computer hours by playing with me online and never judging me for my nonsensical life observations.

Then, this year, it went a step further and super fans (super readers if you prefer) actually banded together and named yourselves: Pillow Fighters. I can't tell you how much I love the playfulness of the name—a bunch of us staying up late, reading, having fun in an endless party where super readers of my work can share and mingle regardless of which hemisphere you're in. (You have to check out the logo Mandy M. Roth made for you all on my website: www.michellepillow.com)

TO MY AUTHOR & INDUSTRY FRIENDS:

Ten Years this April since my first book published in 2004. I can honestly say I would not still be writing if not for Mandy M. Roth. She supported me when real life tried to drown out the fictional voices. She kicked my ass when it needed kicked, as a best friend should. She's more than a friend, she's a sister.

I am very blessed with a community of awesome peers:

Jaycee Clark, from the very beginning you just fit. I can't imagine not knowing you.

Yasmine Galenorn, PPAMP says hi! You make me laugh when we're joking around online and can be serious when the time calls for it. Be on the lookout for a basket full of kittens on your doorstep.

Candace Havens, my work doppelganger. I love your positive attitude and spirit.

Candice Gilmer, you introduced me to real life ghost hunters and helped make a dream come true. And to Cheryl Knight, my editor at Paranormal Underground Magazine, for letting me write about those experiences.

Authors, I have met so many of you over the years, too many to name, but hopefully you know who you are and that you're appreciated.

Heidi Moore and Lesley Parkin, my editor and final line editor on this book, and to the rest of my editors: Your help is invaluable.

Thank you!

1

INTERGALACTIC GAMBLING CHAMPIONSHIP, TORGAN BLACK MARKET

City of Madaga, Planet of Torgan

Riona Grey knew better than to press her luck. Unfortunately, that didn't stop her from opening her mouth to issue perhaps the stupidest challenge she'd ever uttered, "Oh, I know I can win, Range. I'm the best. I could beat your guys blindfolded, after a night spent hallucinating on Torganian Rum and drunk off my ass. In fact, I can take this whole tournament."

Of course, the space pirate had to force her to put her money where her mouth was because she'd said it in front of his entire crew. And, of course, Riona took his bet and tripled it because, well, she was a sucker for high stakes and mischief. Besides, every time Range crossed her path, he pissed her off. He didn't really do anything, but his smarmy, sexist nature rubbed her the wrong way. She saw his smug face and she wanted to hit him. Instead, she continued on to insult his manhood, his ship and, perhaps most wounding of all, his reputation as a space pirate. Apparently, pirate captains didn't like to be called, "second-rate cargo shippers with a puffed-up reputation with only a list of misdemeanor planetary level charges to his credit." That one got a gun pointed in her face and the ante upped to nearly four times the original amount—fifty-thousand space credits.

Good thing she was an expert when it came to gambling, because she didn't have that kind of money.

Good thing she was so close to winning.

Range could lick her boots. It was going to be sweet perfection to see his face as he handed over that many space credits. Adding that to the tournament prizes and she'd be set for life. No more running around taking odd jobs and doing whatever she could to survive. This was it. Her chance.

The tournament was a lock. There was no way she was losing at Frendle's Chips. This was her game. She would walk away with the winnings, an extra fifty-thousand space credits and some of Range's pride. Today was going to be a good day.

Looking up at the glass-and-metal ceiling, she quietly corrected herself, "Tonight is going to be a *great* night." Traveling from planet to planet, living in deep space, it became hard to differentiate night from day. Really, it just depended on where you landed.

Riona loved her life. She loved everything about it. Well, almost everything, but she had seen enough to know better than to complain. Things could always be worse. She could still be starving, fighting for a small corner of a ship so that she could sleep undisturbed. Desperation and necessity had taught her how to survive, and she was good at it. There were no handouts in the universe for people like her.

The loud music, smoky atmosphere and drunken patrons were comforting in their familiarity. She liked how simplistic everyone was on this level of existence. The humanoid and non-humanoid aliens were predictable. They could be expected to uphold certain codes of honor…to a point. They would act in their own self-interest first, the interest of their crew second, and in the interest of breaking the law third.

There was freedom to their tarnished honor. But best of all, none of them had any grand plans beyond amassing more money and having more adventures. They had flown to the ends of the known universes and had seen marvels beyond speech, and yet living creatures in general still managed to debase that beauty. For most of them, life was short and fairly pointless. Disasters happened. Ships exploded. Fortunes were lost. Planets were blown into nothingness. And sometimes, smarmy pirates lost bets to a girl.

Riona smiled at her last opponent, feeling her heartbeat quicken. One play left. That's all she needed. One perfect play and she walked away the tournament winner. She was aware of the stares of those in the complex on her, knew her face was being broadcast in an oversized holographic projection floating above her head so everyone could see. Long, metal tables stretched out before her, most of them occupied with spectators. The smell of liquor exuded from the nearby bar that dominated the center of the building. Smoke filtered along the floor, being drawn to ventilation grates.

Riona reached to the table next to her and made a show of taking an unconcerned drink. In truth, she could barely swallow because her heart was beating so hard. Metal discs floated before her in a large game grid. Tiny snaps of electricity shot between them. She tapped her fingernails against an inert disc as she contemplated her next move. Her mind raced and calculated, making sense of the seemingly random pattern of electrical shocks.

"I hear human women often freeze under pressure," her opponent jeered. He talked in his native language of Yidie, but she understood the scaly lizard man just fine thanks to her implanted universal translator.

Riona laughed a loud, delighted sound as she held up her disc. To herself, she quietly counted, *One, Two, Thr—*

"Ri!"

At the sudden, startling sound, her fingers slipped and the disc went a millimeter off its original course and right into a strip of electricity. For the longest second, her heart stopped beating and her confident smile fell. The unit blinked once and then fizzled as the disc was destroyed. Metal particles fell to the table. Chaos erupted in a series of cheers and pounding fists of protest.

Turning almost numbly to the distraction, she had to blink to be sure she wasn't seeing things. Aeron? What in all the bounty of Jareth was her sister doing here? Now?

Unable to believe her eyes, she stood, consciously forcing the smile back to her lips. She couldn't appear too shaken, not with fifty-thousand space credits now past due and a collector only too willing for an excuse to punish her for reneging. Not to mention it had taken all her savings to enter the tournament.

She was now dead broke and in debt to a pirate.

Lights flashed around them and Aeron ducked her head down to avoid the photographs. She wore the uniformed cap of the Federation Military to hide her black hair. A quick glance down told Riona that Aeron also wore the rest of the get-up. Full military blacks. Why in all the fire surges of Bravon was the military here? And why was her sister the analyst with them?

Eyeing Aeron, Riona said through tight lips, "Greetings, sister. I didn't know the Federation was sending security guards to the event. You should have sent a transmission warning me. I would have told you this wasn't your scene."

"I need to talk to you," Aeron said. Nearly five years since she'd seen the woman in the flesh and it was straight to business. Sure, they had the regular, mandatory family communications, but they didn't seek each other out. In fact, it wouldn't surprise Riona if she learned Aeron denied they were related.

"So serious. Careful, it will wrinkle your face." Riona glanced at her lost game before turning her attention to the last place she'd seen Range and his crew. He was easy to spot with his spiky black hair and dark green facial tattoos scrolled along his cheekbones. The pirate grinned at her and lifted his fingers to wave. Sarcastically, she muttered, "Your timing is as impeccable as always."

"This is bigger than playtime. It's serious," Aeron insisted.

"I can see that," Riona said. Range rested his hand on his gun in warning.

"Would you forget about that stupid game? I need you to come with me. This is important. When was the last time I actually came to you for help?" Aeron did have a point. "You know I wouldn't be here if I had any other choice."

"Where are the other militants?" Riona's expression gave nothing away. She couldn't help but wonder if this was a trap. Had her sister come to arrest her? She was with the ship that had hijacked the cold-storage shipment heading toward Harn, but that had been over four years ago. She'd covered her tracks, hadn't she? There was also that Grooten misunderstanding. Or the bar fight on Valor 6. And she did steal fuel once from a fueling dock on a dare, but she'd been in disguise and the wanted issue had her drawn up to look like a Liphobian sea slug with fur. As far as she could tell, no such creatures actually existed—unless by some horrific misfortune a snowbeast had mated with a Liphobian.

"I'm alone."

"You're here on leave? You left the floating base

to actually take a trip?" For a brief second, Riona thought perhaps her sister had actually learned to loosen the belt straps and have a good time.

"Yes, or I was on leave until… Well, no, not exactly, but once I explain you'll realize I didn't have a choice. This is about—"

Riona lifted her hand to stop her sister from explaining and nodded. The people around them might be pretending to party, but she would bet at least five of them listened to the conversation. In fact, several of them might even get ideas. Those who placed wagers on her wouldn't be too happy at Aeron's interruption. Several of them might go so far as to recoup their losses at the cost of her sister's delicate hide.

"Is this favor off planet?" Riona asked. *Blast the stars.* What was she going to do? She'd been so close.

Fifty. Thousand. Space credits.

Riona found it hard to breathe.

"Yes, but it—"

"Do you have a ship?" Riona interrupted, keeping her voice low. She needed to get off this planet and fast. Range would only hold back for so long.

"Yes."

"Then lead the way. You are family after all." Riona lifted a couple of fingers to Range, motioning that she was going to get his money. He narrowed his eyes, but he didn't immediately move to stop her. She knew he would send men to follow her. He trusted her about as much as she trusted him—and with good reason, she was planning on running out on him without paying. "Who am I to disappoint family?"

Aeron tried to stop walking when Riona would usher her through the crowd. "I have a ship that can get us off planet, but—"

"Yeah, yeah, tell me all about it in flight, sis. We'll have plenty of time to catch up in space." Riona tried not to think about her massive loss. She felt the eyes of the crowd on them, watching. It took all her concentration to smile and act unconcerned.

The crowd was the usual mix of disreputable lowlife creatures one would expect to find in Madaga. Riona knew to stay away from the hired guns and slave traders. However, the pirates, bounty hunters and crooked business men made for decent enough conversation. Though she doubted Aeron would feel the same way. Her sister jerked away from a group of aliens. They looked mostly human but with thick ridges across their foreheads and cheeks. They fanned their webbed hands in front of their faces to create a breeze in the crowded area.

A set of three very hostile eyes met hers. The Pha'n had bet on her to win. One eye stayed on Riona as the other two moved meaningfully to an unsuspecting Aeron. The race had a quick temper, which usually ended up with body parts being dumped in all corners of the galaxy. Riona gave a meaningful nod to the Pha'n woman and then pointed two fingers briefly to the artery in her neck, indicating she was handling it. The Pha'n made no move to follow, but it was clear the restraint took much unnatural effort on her part.

"There's my soldier," a humanoid man in a feather dress said to Aeron as they passed. "Come back to conscript me?"

The blue-skinned creature next to him laughed heartily in a high-pitched whine. "Con-*strip* you!'

"I see you've been making friends," Riona drawled wryly under her breath, eyeing her sister's uniform. Sometimes she didn't think it was possible they came from the same mother.

"I didn't. They harassed me when I came in to find you and—"

"Yeah, you better keep that affronted-military-voice thing down. Pirates don't take kindly to the law," Riona warned. Aeron was always so literal. Was it possible they even came from the same parents? "You're lucky there was a costume ball tonight and that Federation dress is raging this year with the personal entertainment crowd or you'd have been lynched before you could step through the front door."

"I can assure you, Ri, I didn't want to come here. I didn't have a choice. And I can take care of myself." Aeron gasped. "Personal entertain—did you just say I look like a prostitute?"

"What? No," Riona lied, "you misheard." She saw one of Range's thugs following several paces behind. "Well then, let's not make you wait around here too long. Where's that ship of yours, sis? I can't wait to see it." She tried to hurry Aeron along while smiling for the benefit of Range's men. Joner, a hulking piece of roughened manmeat, had a little bit of a thing for her, but that was one disc this gambler didn't want to have to throw.

"Where are you staying? Don't you need to tell your ride that you have other arrangements? Or is there luggage we need to pick up?"

Riona thought of her clothes and meager belongings. Everything she had that was worth fighting for she carried on her person at all times. If she managed to give Range and his men the slip, her room is the first place they'd plunder. Besides, thanks to Aeron's untimely interruption, Riona didn't even have the money to pay her room bill—not that the rusted metal hole in the wall could be considered a real room. "I only flew in for the tournament and didn't bring much with me. I'm all yours. Now where's that ship?"

"What is with you?" Aeron demanded, trying to slow down.

"I'm hurt. My sister comes here after how many years and asks *me* for *my* help and now you suspect I'm up to something because I drop everything to help you?" Riona sighed, shaking her head in disapproval. "It's not like you ask me for favors. The least I can do is take you seriously when you do."

"Well, ah, thank you," Aeron said, nodding slowly. "That is very adult of you, Ri. I can see things have apparently changed with you."

"Riona!"

Riona flinched. Range had apparently changed tactics and decided to follow her himself. They had just walked onto the docking platform where all the ships were parked along an open clearing of concrete. Rows of various travel vessels lined up in assigned squares, packed snugly together to maximize the use of the space. A few people milled about, mostly couples in risqué positions and drunken crewmen trying to find a place to pass out now the gambling was winding down. In the main complex behind them, the party raged on and would continue to do so for several more days. That was the beauty of deep space travel. All the travelers were on a different time schedule, and one person's morning was another person's evening, so when they all gathered together time blended into one long planetary party.

"Should we stop? I think someone's trying to get your attention." Aeron tried to point at the main complex.

"No, I think we should go. Is this your ship? The Federation Military vessel? Subtle, sis, very subtle."

"Riona! I know you're not trying to renege on our bet," Range yelled, the sound of his heavy footfalls coming faster.

"Hey, I think that guy—" Aeron insisted.

"We should really get going, as in now," Riona said, grabbing her sister's arm and jerking her the last several feet to the ship.

"You're in trouble, aren't you? I knew it. I knew you hadn't grown up. You're just using me! I was an idiot to think I could—"

"Do you think we could continue this lecture later? That guy isn't trying to ask me out on a date, if you know what I mean." Her words were punctuated by a warning laser blast aimed in their direction. It whizzed past before fizzling into nothingness.

"Are they shooting at us?" Aeron screamed in surprise as she jerked violently to the left to take cover. "Are they insane? What are they thinking? This is a Federation ship. I am a Federation civilian employee!"

Riona actually laughed at her. How could she not? "Where I come from, that's a reason to shoot. No one will care if you're civilian or military bred. Besides, they're only firing warning shots. They're too far behind us to do much damage to the ship. They just want me to know they're not going to forget the debt so easily."

To Aeron's credit, she hurried to press the security code into the ship's panel to open the entry hatch on the bottom. Instantly, a door slid open and a ladder came down from above. Leading the way, she said, "I can't believe you are so careless with money. I should make you go down and face him."

Riona tolerated the lecture as she followed her sister up the ladder. Only when Aeron stopped to take a breath, did she insert, "Unless you have a bag full of space credits you're willing to leave with me, I'm going to have to beg you not to do that. Besides, you give me a lift and I promise I'll help you with whatever you need." Riona wasn't too worried. Her sister's sense of adventure ran toward a really hard logic puzzle, a cup of hot grog and an auto-warm blankie. How much help could the woman really need?

"How much do you owe?" Aeron demanded, hands on hips as she stopped short of going into the cockpit to start the engines.

Riona hit the control button to make the hatch seal shut. "Don't worry about it." She passed her sister to take the pilot's seat and automatically began initiating launch protocols. A viewing screen popped up to show movement on the outside of the ship as a warning before initiating thrusters. Range was there, slamming his fist into the metal side. His anger reverberated loudly from below. The viewing screen sound was off, but she could see his lips moving and didn't need to hear what he was saying to *know* what he was saying.

"Hey, this is my ship. I'll do the flying."

"Ever out fly an angry pirate?" Riona arched a brow. Aeron gave her a dubious look. "That's what I thought, analyst. Why don't you just strap in and let me handle this boat? The sooner we get out of here, the better our odds of losing him before the chase even starts. And if I know Range, he'll give chase." As if to prove her point, the pirate stopped hitting their ship and turned to run down the docking lot. He disappeared from the viewing screen.

"We come from the same place, you know," Aeron said.

"What are you talking about?" Riona started

up the engine, doing a mental check of the buttons and switches as she readied for flight.

"You said where you come from being Federation is a bad thing. That's not true. We come from the same place." Aeron's literal take on life worked well with her militant pursuits…not so well when trying to relate to other humanoids.

"Yeah," Riona drawled absentmindedly, jerking the controls, "a giant minefield of floating rock."

"Our home world was lovely," Aeron defended.

"Until it exploded into a thousand pieces," Riona answered. "I flew near there a few years back. Nothing but blackness. Even most of the meteors seemed to have floated away."

"How can you talk about it like that?"

Riona didn't answer as she brought up the map of Torgan. Three rings spun at odd angles around the brown-gray planet. Grabbing the communicator, she said, "Torgan Ground, this is, ah—" Riona glanced around trying to find a name and then settled for, "—a ship and we're about to take off, so if you don't want us exploding over the docking platform you better clear the air."

"Riona!" Aeron scolded.

"A ship this is Torgan Ground. We need a little more…" The communicator's words faded as Riona turned down the volume and concentrated on getting out of there.

"What?" She feigned innocence as she began the final phases of departure procedures. The ship was a little different than she was used to, but at this point she could fly just about anything as long as it wasn't a giant cruiser or space station. She wasn't too worried. She knew enough about Torgan to know they wouldn't want a ship exploding over their docking lot. They would be liable not only for ruined ships and damage to their facility, but they'd have possible authoritative inquiries into the incident.

Aeron grabbed the communicator and turned the volume back up. "My apologies for the rookie, Torgan Ground. She panicked. This is Federation ship class three cruiser number six-nineteen-twenty requesting you open for an emergency takeoff." Glancing at her sister, she said, "We've got a level nineteen prisoner onboard that we'd like to get out of your sky."

"Federation class three, understood. Clearing sky traffic. You have an open shot into deep space. Scan protocols being activated and ships are being locked down."

"The Federation thanks you for your cooperation, Torgan Ground," Aeron said, shutting the communicator off.

"Level nineteen prisoner?"

"Possible toxic contaminate," Aeron answered.

"Wow, thanks for that," Riona drawled sarcastically, realizing her sister had likened her to infectious waste. Though she had called Aeron a prostitute earlier, so she guessed they were even. "I love you too."

"I just did you a favor. Whoever is chasing you will have to wait for contamination clearance. Standard protocol whenever there is a possible onworld level nineteen contamination."

The ship shook as they began to move. "I'll have to remember that. Thanks for the tip."

"I didn't tell you that so you would—"

Riona purposefully jerked the ship, jarring her sister to the right and then left to get the woman to stop talking. It worked. Aeron stopped lecturing her. "Try to hold on there, sis."

Lights began to blur on the viewing screen and the ride became smoother. She relaxed some as the surface view faded from the sensors.

"I can't believe you, Ri," Aeron said through gritted teeth. "I'm with you for two seconds and we're already being chased off a planet because you owe money to a space pirate…"

Blarg. Blarg. Blarg. Riona moved her mouth, silently mocking the lecture and not really paying attention to it. She pushed several buttons before turning away from the control panel to let the ship guide itself. "Okay, you got me out here. We're in space. What's so important you had to slum it with the lowlifes?"

"I need your help. I have to get to a planet on the outer edge of the Y quadrant. I can't keep this ship."

Riona arched a brow.

"The planet is called Qurilixen. The Federation has no authority there, and quite frankly little interest in it or the people, but for their mining operations. The Draig and Var people who inhabit the planet keep to themselves and by all reports live quite primitively. About five months ago, I intercepted some data that leads me to believe the people there might be in trouble. The Federation refused to get involved. So long as they get the ore mined on the planet one way or another, they're keeping their hands clean of the whole situation. But after seeing our home world explode, I can't stand by and watch another race of people get wiped out—especially over something like mining rights. If something happened and I did nothing—"

"So let me get this straight," Riona interrupted. "You left work without permission and you stole a Federation ship, which you now need to ditch because you're heading to a primitive planet in the Y and don't want the military tracking you. And you need my help to get you there."

"Yes." Aeron bit her lip and nodded. "Will you help me?"

A slow smile spread over Riona's lips. "Ah, little sis, I'm so proud right now I might start crying. Of course I'll help you break a bunch of Federation laws." And the fact Range wouldn't dream of looking for her in the Y was a bonus. "Besides, you know me. I'm always up for a little mischief and adventure."

Riona wasn't sure if her sister's resulting expression was grateful or an attempt to hide her disapproval.

FINDING a ship that was going immediately to the outer regions of the Y quadrant, to a primitive planet called Qurilixen that rarely allowed anyone to land on its soil, and a ship that also happened to be landing on the half of the planet that was inhabited by the Draig and not the half inhabited by a race called the Var, proved to be surprisingly easy. One hacked database search later and Riona had such a ship. It was taking passengers. It was close enough for them to reach in the stolen Federation cruiser and if they flew smart they would have enough fuel to land. And, best of all, it wouldn't cost them a single space credit to get onboard the luxury craft. If she believed in the gods of fate, she'd say they were smiling at them right now—or they really didn't like Range.

Glancing to the chair next to her where her sister insisted on sleeping, she frowned. Unfortunately, there was one very big, very un-Aeron-approved catch. In order to hitch a ride, they had to be contracted as potential brides.

Assured that Aeron slept, Riona pulled up the Galaxy Brides advertisement she'd found in a magazine chip and read to herself, *"Wanted: Galaxy Brides Corporation seeking 46 fertile humanoid-compatible females of early childbearing years and A5+ health status for marriage to strong, healthy Qurilixian males at their annual Breeding Festival. Possibility of royal attendance. Must be eager bed partners, hard workers. Virginity a plus. Apply with official health documents, travel papers and IQ screen to: Galaxy Brides, Phantom Level 6, X Quadrant, Earthbase 5792461."*

The Earthbase was close and, by the departure date listed on the screen, they could just make it. Luckily, the corporation seemed more worried about filling a quota than the actual screening process. They accepted the forged documents Riona transmitted to them from her counterfeit ID papers. Pulling up her sister's documents proved to be a little trickier, but she managed. A forged signature later and they were in business. Within seconds, Galaxy Brides confirmed their booking with a long welcome letter and assurances they'd made the right decision for their future happiness.

Riona thought it best not to mention the details to her sister until it became an unavoidable conversation. There was no reason to get Aeron all worked up about the trip. She would never admit it, but the moment Aeron had mentioned the possible destruction of a planet, a knot had formed inside her, constructed partly of memory, partly of fear and partly of an overwhelming sense of helpless need.

Riona had witnessed the end of her home world, and since Aeron had showed up, the nightmares of it had come back. She looked at her sister, wishing more than anything the woman had kept her distance. But now that Aeron was here, Riona couldn't turn her away. If there was a planet in trouble, she couldn't ignore it. Aeron wouldn't approve of Riona's methods, but it was the only way she could think of to help. And maybe, just maybe, if she helped stop this disaster the nightmares of her past would never come back.

Galaxy Brides spaceship, six weeks later.

"Oh, come on! Seriously, why else would the

Qurilixian men call their wedding ceremony a *Breeding Festival*? It is so laughably obvious. It has nothing to do with love and everything to do with a planet full of horny males, with no females of their own, who need to find release," Olena announced, continuing her ongoing monologue about their future *husbands*. The more Olena drank, the funnier she became. Riona liked her. A lot.

The woman had the most brilliant flaming-red hair—much brighter than Riona's auburn locks, the sides of which were pulled up into a center knot to cascade down her back in curls. Riona had admired the hairpin sticking out of it, only to be told that Olena used it to handle her business—code for the hairpin was tipped in poison. It was then Riona knew they were of the same mold.

Unlike her stuffy sister, who hid out in her luxury room for most of the trip through the stars, Riona had found a small group of potential brides that were a little more her speed. If she didn't know better, she'd say this Olena Leyton was much more than she let on. Riona didn't care. The woman was allowed her secrets, even if they were of a piratical sort.

They were lounging on the floor of her luxury suite on the Galaxy Brides spaceship. The rest of the prospective brides were getting ready for the official docking the next evening. The women were quarantined from the crew to ensure nothing unseemly happened, which caused some of the women to jokingly refer to their quarters as the harem.

Olena began to hum. Riona laughed, recognizing the old pirate drinking song.

"And we sail the high skies looking for gold," Olena sang softly.

"Looking for treasures that never grow old," Riona added, louder.

Olena laughed to discover her new friend knew the words and they both instantly burst into drunken concert, "The wind in our sails, lads, the stars at our feet, as we plunder for women, thick brown and good mead!"

They fell over laughing, barely able to get the last part out.

Riona had spent the last month being pampered and primped. Personal droids were assigned to each room. There were cooking units in each of their quarters that could materialize almost any culinary delight. She readily admitted she loved everything about the ride. Who wouldn't? Massages and manicures, pedicures and servants… Plus, the ship had a medic unit. Free health maintenance.

Happiness and bliss. Happiness and bliss.

Riona's stomach hurt from laughing. She fell to the side, dropping her arm before tossing her disc at the game board. It slid off course and was electrocuted into dust. She laughed harder.

Smirking, Olena continued, "These dopey brides actually think they're going to marry royalty. I mean, the whole rumor about there being four princes going to attend is just an advertising technique to get women to sign up. They'll probably end up with farmers and servants. There has to be a reason the Draig don't let the people talk to each other before the ceremony. My guess, the men are stupid. The best we can hope for is they shut up and look pretty. Yeah, like anyone ever found true love at the end of a glowing crystal."

"Glowing crystal?" Riona interrupted.

"Yeah, you know about the crystals, right?"

Riona shook her head in denial. "I didn't get around to the whole wedding ceremony uploads, just the planetary survival facts." Mainly because she had no intention of going through with an archaic ceremony. Once they told the right person why they were there, surely Riona and her sister would be excused from the whole contracted marriage thing.

Out of boredom, Riona had taken advantage of some of the basic Qurilixen uploads. The process worked using the ship's computer to load information directly into the brain. It made universal understanding a lot easier and more efficient. Riona had researched practical things—the planet, the people, a general sense of where they were going in the universe on the off chance she had to steal a ship and escape.

Olena motioned to her neck, absently waving her finger back and forth. "They wear the crystals around their necks and, when they look at their future woman, the rock starts to glow. Apparently, it reacts to their level of horniness of something."

"You're joking," Riona drawled skeptically.

"Maybe about the horniness levels part," Olena admitted, chuckling as she lifted her glass of Old Earth whiskey to her lips. Taking a drink, she sputtered a little and said, "This stuff is surprisingly good…after you're drunk of course and really can't taste it anymore."

"What are medic units for if not to cure a hangover," Riona answered. She too lifted a glass of whiskey to her lips and coughed lightly at the initial sip before swallowing a mouthful of the hard liquor. "These food simulators really do make anything."

"Too bad they can't materialize space credits. Wouldn't that be something? I'd buy this ship and kick everyone off, you and the pilots not included."

"Thanks." Riona lifted her glass.

Olena studied her liquor thoughtfully and mused, "I suppose it's easy for the Draig to say I love you to one of the only women on the entire planet."

Riona followed the changing conversation with ease. "How else are the poor bastards going to get a little happy-happy for their little happies?"

Qurilixen was inhabited by primitive males similar to Viking clans of Medieval Old Earth—not that Riona knew too much about Old Earth. Some scientist theorized that many of the humanoids had started on Old Earth long, long ago because of some genetic similarities, but Riona wasn't much for science. Ancient history was just that—history. Today is what mattered.

The Draig race worshipped many gods, favored natural comforts to modern technical conveniences and preferred to cook their own food without the aid of a simulator. They were classified as warriors, though they had been peaceful for nearly a century—aside from petty territorial skirmishes that broke out every fifteen or so years between a few of the rival houses. All in all, it sounded rather dull.

"If you're so against this marriage," Riona said, "why are you here?"

"I wanted breast enlargements," Olena answered, her face serious. She puffed out her chest against the cotton robe. "But Gena's been in the machine for the last week growing her two-ton rocket blasters and I can't get an appointment."

Riona instantly burst into another fit of laughter. She gasped for breath, reaching for her whiskey glass on the floor next to her. Gena wasn't well liked on the ship and was often avoided. The woman was annoying, thinking and talking only of herself and her new breast enhancements.

The sound of the door sliding open caught her attention and both women turned to see who'd interrupted. Aeron stood staring at them, arms crossed.

"Speaking of two-ton rocket blasters," Olena mumbled, pushing to her feet. She wobbled but didn't fall. "I should go before you two explode and take out half the ship."

Riona saw her sister's tight expression and felt the laughter draining out of her. Aeron wasn't exactly pleased with Riona's method of getting her to Qurilixen and she had made her displeasure known every time they crossed paths. Okay, admittedly, Riona should have perhaps told her sister what was going on *before* she had her on the bridal ship and in deep space. Honestly, she kind of thought Aeron would have noticed the giant wedding banner as they boarded the ship.

"Are you drunk?" Aeron demanded.

"Apparently not enough," Riona mumbled as Olena left them alone. She ambled to her feet, bumping the playing board. Some of her unused discs skidded along the floor. Instantly, a cleaning droid activated and began attending to the mess. She stepped around the machine to get to the bed. All around them was every starship convenience known to humanoids —beauty droids, cosmetic enhancements, food simulators that could materialize almost anything they desired and an oversized bed to pass out on.

"I can't believe you're drinking. I thought we'd made plans to get together to discuss our plans once we land."

"Plans for making plans," Riona mumbled, adding sarcastically, "Yep, that sounds like me, Federation. I'm a planner."

"Gah!" Aeron threw up her arms. "Why are you always like this? I can't even have a simple conversation with you. And I told you, don't call me Federation."

"Listen, *Federation*." Riona sat, wanting nothing more than to fall against the mattress and into oblivion. She saw no point in worrying about tomorrow when today was to be lived. "I have a plan. We arrive tomorrow with the other brides. We blend in so we can be assured of getting off this ship without any incident. From what I gathered, we get off the ship, are presented before the potential husbands, attend a party, eat, drink, be merry, and maybe get a little happy-happy with the locals if they're cute."

"I am *not* getting a little happy-happy or anything else with the locals," Aeron swore.

"Suit yourself. I hear they're sexy." Riona shrugged. "If you change your mind, I've got an extra set of transmitters."

"You actually think the primitive people are going to want to use transmitters to exchange pleasure essences?" Aeron laughed, the sound mocking and a little bitter. Riona stiffened. "Seriously, Ri? I don't know if you've noticed, but universal men tend to want the real thing. You might get someone to try it out of mere curiosity, but do you really think when they find out what our heritage is they're going to want spend the night with either of us? We don't react like normal women. The only men in the galaxies who understood that little fact exploded."

"So you haven't..." Riona asked.

"And start the clock ticking? I think not. I haven't met anyone worth dying for."

"Well—" Riona swallowed, uncomfortable with the course of the conversation, "—I haven't either and I'm not going to. Not until I collect on those fifty-thousand space credits I figure you owe me."

"*What?*"

"It's your fault I lost that match. Now I can't go

back to Torgan, or half the other haunts I enjoy, for a very long time. Range will be sure to tell everyone I reneged on our bet."

"Would you stop blaming me for your gambling?" Aeron snorted in disgust.

"I didn't ask you to come to Torgan. You did that on your own. You came to me." Riona glared at her sister. This is why they didn't talk. Every conversation seemed to detonate a full-blown fight.

"I told you I'm trying to save a planet," Aeron said. "I'm sorry if I think that's slightly more important than your game."

Unable to stay upright, Riona lay back on the bed and stared at the metal ceiling. The weld lines blurred in a drunken haze. "You know, I don't even think you've thanked me for getting you on this ship. All you've done is complain the whole ride."

"I will not let what happened to our home world happen to the people of Qurilixen." Aeron must have realized Riona's irritation over the mention of their home world, because she instantly lightened her tone. "This isn't just about our childhood home. This is about a planet that needs saving. If the Tyoe succeed in their plans, they will kill everyone over mining rights. I can't let the Draig race become exterminated when I can try to stop it."

"We," Riona stated, still studying the ceiling

grates. "*We* will not let it happen. Listen, we go, we smile, we pretend to consider our options, we drink, we dance or whatever it is these Draigs do for fun, and then you do what you have to and we leave. If something unexpected happens, we deal with it. There is the plan. Simple and easy to remember. I'm sure if you ask around, you'll find whoever is in charge of the mines. Just don't be late getting back to the ship in the morning. All the unchosen brides are guaranteed a ride back and we don't have the money to pay for another way offworld. I'll meet you here and we'll slip away as soon as the boat docks somewhere inhabitable and I'll get to work deleting our contracts out of the Galaxy Brides system. It will be as if this never happened."

Silence answered her, but Riona didn't open her eyes to look. A long moment passed. She imagined Aeron glaring at her, ready to explode. Instead, the door slid open. Quietly, Aeron said, "Thank you, Ri."

Riona looked over in surprise, just in time to see the door sliding shut behind her sister.

2

LITHOR REPUBLIC AMBASSADORIAL SPACECRAFT, PLANET OF QURILIXEN'S OUTER ORBIT

Lord Miroslav, Ealdorman of Draig, absently watched as his home world passed across the viewing portal. Mountains and forest seemed to meld seamlessly together, so small he could block the entire planet from his eye line with both hands. Absently, he drew his finger along his line of vision, tracing what would be the route he'd soon travel from his home in the northern mountains to the Draig royal palace where the upcoming Breeding Festival was to be held. The path reminded him of the curve of a woman's hip.

From the sky, Qurilixen appeared reddish-brown, but where he lived in the mountains, the earth was red with streaks of gray. Though he couldn't see it, he knew exactly where his castle home lay nestled in a valley. It gave him some comfort to know the fortress was hidden from view, virtually undetectable from space.

Here on the ship in his duties as Mining Ambassador, he was Lord Miroslav, but at home with his three brothers, he was simply Mirek. He preferred being Mirek. His family was everything to him. Unfortunately, family consisted of merely the four noble brothers. Mirek's parents were no longer living. None of the brothers had been blessed with a wife and consequently had no children.

From space, there were no shadows over the land as the suns hit the surface at different angles. The temperatures on the planet were moderate to warm, though it could get cold in the highest mountains. Near the royal palace at the base of the mountains, the earth was a dark red and filled with nutrients to support the colossal trees of the southern forest. With three suns, the planet received a lot of light. Some of the vegetation was so large that the space craft he was on could fit inside a hollowed-out tree trunk.

The two yellow suns were great for the plants, but the radiation from the blue sun affected the people. Radiation altered the men's genetics and made Qurilixian-born women rare. Maybe one in a thousand births was a Qurilixian female. If not for bridal trade, his people would have gone extinct generations back.

Marriage was a complicated matter. The fact they had no women of their own was why the services of corporations like Galaxy Brides were so invaluable. In return for Galaxy Brides arranging the screening and transportation of women willing to marry a stranger, his people mined a specialized ore needed to make high-quality ship fuel. Since the Draig rarely left the planet and didn't use land-crafts to get around, they didn't really have a practical use for the ore.

The next marriage festival was soon, and Mirek was duty bound to attend, and to keep attending year after long year until he found a wife. This was to be his fourth ceremony. Such continual bad luck did not make him look forward to another failed attempt. Like all men, he wanted a wife, yearned for one. It was their duty to marry and have children, to carry on the family name and the Draig culture.

If Mirek was honest with himself, he would admit he wanted more than to carry on the family line. He wanted the entire experience of having a woman. Sex he'd had, but it had been meaningless physical exertions with offworld travelers. He wanted more. He wanted a woman that would wake up beside him, whisper his name, laugh with him, honor him with sons, grace him with smiles and soft touches and…

Mirek frowned, not allowing his thoughts to drift to such things. The gods had not blessed him. Nor had they blessed his brothers. It was a dark shadow that hung over his family's honor. It was quite possible his family line would end with his generation.

For his eldest brother, Bron, this year marked his seventh attempt at finding a bride. Undoubtedly, the High Duke would be in a vile mood during the festivities. The second oldest, Alek, faced his fifth attempt. That left the youngest, Vladan. It was Vlad's first year. Mirek almost felt bad for his little brother. He could remember well the hope and excitement that had filled him during his first festival. There was no reason to believe that Vlad's luck would be any different than his siblings when it came to a life mate.

One unintentional blessing on this year was that his four royal cousins, the Draig princes, would be searching for their brides for the first time. Their royal attendance would take the notice from Mirek's family.

The very idea of a lonely marriage ceremony made him tired.

"It is well you speak, Lord Miroslav, Ealdorman of Draig. We agree to your proposal to send a proposal to your royal family for consideration of our terms for the agreement held herein."

At the steady, soft voice, Mirek turned. He let all thoughts of marriage fade from his mind as he concentrated on his duties. The Lithorian people were a tedious race, small in stature and great in manners. It had taken Mirek years of training to learn just the basic Lithorian etiquettes. However, it was worth it. They produced the best chocolate in the galaxy and every female on the planet practically went crazy for just a taste of it.

Mirek averted his eyes to the left, bent his head to the side and answered, "By the graces of the Lithorian people, I thank you on behalf of my people the Draig, Barun Monke of the Lithor." Mirek reached out his hands, palms facing up. A thick stack of parchment was placed on them.

"The proposal document, Lord Miroslav, Ealdorman of Draig," the barun said.

"By the graces of the Lithorian people, I thank you again, Barun Monke. I will personally deliver this into the hands of Prince Olek, the Draig Royal Ambassador."

Mirek did not envy his cousin, the prince. The

proposal would just be the first of several hundred pages worth of negotiations that would basically end up being a simple straight trade, *Galaxa-promethium* ore for chocolate.

"As agreed," the barun acknowledged. "The airlock is being initiated between our two ships if you are ready to follow me, Lord Miroslav, Ealdorman of Draig."

"By the graces of the Lithorian people, I thank you again, Barun Monke." Mirek sighed, trying to fight the headache forming behind his right eye. It was the same headache he received any time he had to deal with these particular negotiators. Too bad today's appointment wasn't a stranded Galaxy Playmate ship filled with beautiful, lonely, unmated women. What better distraction to take his mind from the upcoming disappointment of yet another failed ceremony?

Gods' bones, he missed the feel of soft flesh and sweet lips—even if it was merely a physical release. Fleeting pleasures were better than no pleasure at all.

Breeding Festival Grounds, near the Draig Palace, planet of Qurilixen

Riona winked at the Galaxy Brides crewman.

Though the entire section set aside for brides was automated to ensure the bridal cargo arrived uncompromised, the workers flying the spacecraft were not. It hadn't taken much to hack into the system via a beauty droid's interior drive and strike up a conversation with a crewman, which had led to a game of chance, which had led to a natural win, which had led to Riona getting a private exit off the ship away from the parade of brides.

"Thank you, Charl," she said. "Remember to watch your mouth. It gives your hand away every time."

"If you're not looking for a husband, I could give my mouth away to you," the man offered.

Riona laughed. "Better gamblers have tried. Trust me, I'm the kind of trouble a man like you can't handle."

"You are probably right, especially when you're wearing a dress like that. See you on the return flight for a rematch." He grinned and closed the maintenance hatch, leaving her alone on the primitive alien planet.

Riona smiled. Charl's mouth wasn't his only tell. Once she trounced him on the return trip, she'd make sure he deleted Aeron's and her name from Galaxy Brides' database.

The crew was doing a bio scan to make sure none of the brides had tried to get out of their duty by hiding on the ship. Even if she could have, Riona hadn't wanted to stay onboard. There was too much fun to be had on a new planet. Besides, the idea of Aeron walking between two rows of sexy barbarian men intent on marriage was going to be something worth seeing. Just the idea made Riona laugh.

To blend in with the other women while waiting for her private exit, Riona had to dress like potential brides in the fine gauze and silk of the traditional Qurilixian gown. The slinky material stirred against her body when she moved, hugging her hips as the skirt flowed around her legs in thin strips. The shoes were soft, almost too soft for walking on the unpaved ground. Running on the local terrain would be hard, not that she had any intention of making a go for the nearby forest. Luckily, it was warm, because the gown's bodice had been cut low to make the most of her breasts without showing her nipples. Normally, she wasn't one for wearing dresses, but the gown didn't bother her. Riona liked disguises.

What she didn't like very much was the way arm straps stretched across her back like long cuffs to keep her wrists tied together. The straps were secured by the way they wound up her forearms and fastened over her elbows. She had enough freedom of movement to reach in front of her, but she couldn't lift her arms over her head and if she tried to strike out, the silken chains would stop her.

Dusk claimed the small planet, turning the earth into a dark and brilliant red. Apparently, this world only had one night of darkness a year, which made the Breeding Festival special. But she'd heard of stranger customs than only allowing marriages to happen in the dark by the light of a glowing crystal.

Riona found it easy to get her bearings as the ship faced a valley filled with pyramid-shaped tents decorated with waving banners. A single large moon shone overhead. Bonfires cast light over the valley, seeming to set it on fire. She loved the earthy primitiveness of it.

Grinning mischievously to no one in particular as she was alone, Riona began to dance to the distant music, hidden by the shadows of the ship. Tonight was going to be so much fun.

"Tonight is a serious matter," Elder Bochman stated. It was his usual speech, one Mirek had had the unhappy pleasure of memorizing. "For those of you fortunate enough to be blessed with a bride, it will be one of the hardest nights of your life."

At the reference to *hard*, a few of the men

chuckled. Bochman arched a brow until they quieted their juvenile reaction.

"We are the Draig," Bochman said. He let his eyes shift with the gold of his dragon form to give the statement more meaning. "We are strong. We are brave. We act on instinct. Put a battle before us, and we will fight it. Put a traitorous Var in front of us, and we will kill him like the stinking cat-shifter he is. No one doubts your bravery, my fellow Draig, but tonight you will be tested beyond all limits. You must fight your instincts, fight your innermost desires and abstain from claiming the one thing you will want more than any other thing in your life."

The potential grooms gave a gruff cheer. Mirek lowered his eyes to the ground. Absently, he touched the sacred crystal hanging around his neck. On the day he was born, his father had journeyed to Crystal Lake, dove beneath the waves and pulled the stone he now wore from the lakebed. Mirek, like all Draig, had worn the crystal ever since. But it wasn't just a custom. It was how they received the will of the gods. When he saw his bride, the crystal would glow, signifying his destiny.

The men cheered louder, drawing Mirek's eyes back up. He knew they were excited, but he could hardly be expected to cheer for a night that would undoubtedly prove fruitless.

As the grooms were directed to make their way

to the receiving lines, Mirek followed his oldest brother, Bron, toward the side of the festival grounds. The familiar music and laughter of his people sounded behind him. Married couples watched on as those too young to participate posed and shouted behind the grooms.

As was tradition, he wore a loincloth, a gold band around his biceps, a black leather mask to hide his face from forehead to upper lip and the sacred crystal necklace. Though they teased, his people were hardly ashamed of the naked form. Unlike the grooms, the onlookers wore the more commonplace tunic.

The grooms stopped, forming two lines as they faced each other. The brides would walk between them for the pairings. Mirek took his place and waited.

Perhaps this year would be different. Perhaps this would be the year they all found brides. Mirek hated hope, and yet here he was feeling it. Bonfires cast the area into stark relief, but he didn't need the firelight to see. As a shifter, his eyes could easily pick out the brides waiting within the open mouth of the Galaxy Brides luxury ship. He focused on each woman, waiting for a spark to snap inside of him, some hint that he would be lucky. Nothing happened.

"I would rather face battle," Mirek said to Bron. "This anticipation is torture."

Bron nodded in agreement. "I cannot believe our little brother does not have to stand in even one of these greeting lines. It is almost laughable that Vladan found his wife before his first ceremony started, and here we are again."

"Aye," Mirek answered, chuckling though he felt no humor.

Before the ceremony, the king had ordered they be presented to a marriageable daughter of a friend of an alien dignitary. Apparently, Lady Clara of the Redding was above attending their *primitive* festival and refused to marry beneath her station. She'd barely even acknowledged them, showing absolutely no emotion on her face. In fact, when Vlad's crystal had glowed, she'd merely nodded, turned her back on them and left the tent. Mirek would never say it out loud, but he was glad Clara was not meant to be his bride, and he felt sorry for Vlad.

Mirek continued, "I do not envy him that bride. I only hope that was paint on her body and not her true flesh. She will scare the children and deliver them into nightmares."

"I did not see the paint. I was too busy staring at her head. Do you think that tower of hair hides a skull beneath it?" Bron asked.

"Our nephews will be born with skulls the shape of pyramids." Mirek was hardly concerned. It would be unfortunate if the only heirs to his family line were deformed in such a way, but he knew he shouldn't question the judgment of the gods—especially on this night.

His brother kept talking, and Mirek automatically answered, though he did not pay attention to what was said. The women had begun to make their way from the ship toward them. That thin thread of hope tried to surface inside him when the first one stepped forward. He studied the female faces as they moved past, and with each opportunity he felt absolutely nothing. No stirring inside him. No connection. No piercing need to claim one of them as his own. Sure, they were pretty, and he'd gladly spend the night in their beds enjoying physical pursuits, but there was nothing to indicate they were his mate. Then, as the last bride made her way through the line, he looked down to his chest to see his crystal resting dormant against his flesh. He was not blessed.

The ache that swelled within him was almost too much to bear. It started in his chest and radiated from his heart into the rest of him. Tension gathered along the back of his neck and shoulders. The world became dull and bleak. It had happened again. What had he done to deserve such treatment from the gods? He worked hard. He did his duty to his people. He lived a fair and just life. He fought against the Var whenever his uncle, the king, commanded it of him. What more could he do?

What more could he do?

What more can I do?

Mirek swallowed against the lump forming in his throat, resisting the urge to scream. There was nothing more he could do. He was cursed to be alone.

Seeing the grooms beginning to move from their lines, he glanced at Bron. His brother's crystal glowed, pulsing with light. He quickly turned his attention to the far end of the line where Alek waited. He too had a glowing crystal. A quick assessment told him that his four prince cousins were also so blessed. Four cousins, all three brothers, all blessed. Mirek was the only one without a mate. The only one.

Alone.

What more could I have done?

The lump came back, this time to settle permanently in his chest. He had to be happy for his family, and he would be…eventually. But right now, in this moment of supreme disappointment, he could barely muster the smile he needed to congratulate all of them on their good fortune. It was one thing to be alone together, but now in light of his brothers' good fortune, Mirek was really and truly alone.

Why do the gods deny me? What more could I have done?

RIONA WAITED for the first of the brides to walk by her hiding spot before slipping into line to go to the feast set out on a raised platform. It had been easy to walk through the festival grounds while everyone's attention had been diverted toward the visiting ship. Riona was only too glad to avoid the mating part of the ceremony. The last thing she wanted was some barbarian taking a liking to her, especially when she got a closer look at them. Bronzed warriors with the bodies of genetically enhanced soldiers weren't exactly the most manageable type. Guys like Charl, she could manipulate because there was absolutely no attraction on her part. And if manipulation didn't work, she could take them in a fight. But these barbarians? Trained warriors who'd probably come by their talents completely naturally? No, thank you. It was best to avoid trouble before it started.

How strange life was. She should have been enjoying her fifty-thousand space credits. Instead, she was deep in debt, hiding out on a primitive planet…with her sister. Her *sister*.

Riona gave a short laugh. Aeron on this planet was worth seeing. Her tidy, uptight sister would probably run back to the ship screaming. She just wished the sight wasn't costing her fifty-thousand space credits.

Fifty-thousand. Where in the galaxy was she going to find that kind of money? Her laugh faded into a frown. Not that she'd let on, but she was in some serious trouble. When word got out that she'd reneged on her bet to Range—and he would make sure everyone heard about it—she wouldn't be trusted on any jobs. Her credit was shot. Without high-dollar games or any somewhat legitimate work, she wouldn't be able to get her cash up.

The sound of music and cheering drew her from her thoughts. Riona wasn't one to dwell on what couldn't be changed. Seeing her home world explode had been a hard lesson, and after that nothing else had really compared.

Riona liked these alien people. They seemed wholesome. Not many planets would turn their backs on scientific and technological advancements.

Seeing her sister in the procession of brides, her head down and her steps short and stunted, Riona laughed. Aeron looked absolutely mortified.

Riona wondered if her sister had even seen a half-naked male in the flesh, so to speak. Aeron had spent all her time stuck in a small room looking at uploads, keeping herself isolated from other life forms. In a way, Riona understood it. Aeron chose to isolate herself to keep from getting too close to anyone. It was a way of protecting herself from the pain of what had happened. Riona chose to do the opposite, surrounding herself with life and distractions to keep from thinking about such things. Life was hard and brutal and unfair, and she was going to squeeze every ounce of pleasure from it she could before it killed her. The only way to ensure she lived was to make herself feel alive. Otherwise, she was nothing and had nothing, and that emptiness would fill her until she choked on it.

The crowd quieted. Seeing the veil over Aeron's upswept black hair, Riona frowned. She'd forgotten to wear her short veil. Hopefully, no one would notice. A servant moved by the table with a pitcher of wine. Riona held out her goblet for him to fill.

"What is it?" she asked him.

The man grinned. "Maiden's Last Breath."

Riona tossed back her head and laughed. "Ha! That is priceless. I love this place."

Seeing her good humor, the man's grin widened. He motioned toward the food laid out in trenchers along the wooden table. "Eat. Drink. You are most welcome, my lady."

Not one to turn down a free meal, Riona helped herself to the roasted two-horned pig meat and Qurilixian blue bread with whipped cheese. The wine tasted sweet, almost too sweet, but with a name like Maiden's Last Breath, she couldn't resist partaking of it. Other than the sweetness, she actually liked the alien food. Real food had more flavor than the stuff that came out of a simulator.

Riona thoroughly enjoyed herself. The brides whispered and giggled as they filled the table and joined in the feasting. Some flirted with the handsome servants. The belt that held her wrists down made maneuvering hard. She let one of the servants place food in her mouth when she was unable to reach across the table for herself.

The low, euphoric rhythm of music wound over her senses. The Draig knew how to celebrate—food, liquor, bonfires, half-naked men. When the handsome grooms appeared to claim their brides, their chosen women obeyed with little protest. Riona didn't understand it. Okay, so in theory she understood the desire to be with one man for the rest of her life, but she didn't get how these women could simply choose a guy based on a glowing crystal and a two-second evaluation. They didn't know anything about their new partners. The grooms could be the rumored princes of the planet or servants or farmers or soldiers. They could be psychotic, or liars, or cheaters, or pirates. They could be diseased, or abusers, or into some really strange sexual practices. And the grooms had no way of knowing what kind of crazy they were apt to marry when they took the alien brides. So much blind faith. So many arranged marriages.

The last of the men came to the table. Instead of choosing a bride, he walked the length only to stop in front of Aeron. His crystal necklace glowed brilliantly, more so when he was near Riona's sister. Aeron and this man? No. It couldn't be. Aeron knew the price of finding someone to physically mate with. Playing and flirting was one thing, but it wasn't Aeron's thing. Riona's smile faltered a little before she caught herself. She forced a laugh she didn't feel, waiting for Aeron to send the man away.

Aeron *would* send the man away, wouldn't she?

The man touched Aeron's cheek and urged her to follow him. Riona's eyes met her sister's. If Aeron so much as blinked in hesitation, Riona would jump over the table and save her. Her body tensed, ready. Riona forced a bigger smile and pretended to laugh at something the woman next to her said. Her smile faded as Aeron disappeared down an earthen path toward the tents. A servant came to her, trying to engage her in conversation. Riona frowned at him, waving him away.

She stared into the distance, waiting for Aeron to reappear. She didn't.

Well played, Aeron, making me think you'd get married. Ha, ha. Joke's over. Come back now. Riona swallowed, silently willing her sister to her. *Come back. You got your payback for me not telling you about the ship being a bridal one. Any second now…*

"My ladies, we thank you for your attendance," a woman announced. If the man waiting behind her was any indication, she was one of the married natives. "Please, enjoy the celebration and be on the Galaxy Brides ship by the rising of the sun."

A few of the women immediately went to board the ship. One woman started to cry at her bad luck. Riona numbly stood, not feeling much like celebrating. Her sister had chosen a man.

As she made her way through the campground, staying along the edges of the festival, Riona passed a few of the unmated grooms. Fur loincloths clung to masculine hips. Golden bands of intricate design clasped around sinewy biceps. From their solid necks hung crystals bound with leather straps. Firelight glistened on their oiled bodies. The Quril-ixian males were every inch the proud warrior class they were rumored to be, some even seemed to tower nearly seven feet tall in height. She could see the appeal, but to marry one? To give up a long life for a night of passion?

"Don't do it, Aeron," Riona whispered, unsure which tent her sister had disappeared into. For all their fighting, Riona didn't wish her sister dead. "Don't leave me to spend an eternity alone in this universe."

3

Dawn came in a soft green haze of diffused light. Riona had watched most of the night for her sister to embark on the Galaxy Brides ship. Aeron hadn't gotten on. Now, as the ship's crew made the last calls for boarding, Riona had a decision to make. She could take her one and only ride off the planet, or she could find Aeron. Her sister had asked only for a way to Qurilixen, nothing more. Riona could technically leave with a clear conscience.

She watched the docking plank lift and heard the engines engage. Soon, the ship broke atmosphere and Riona still stood on the red earth of the primitive planet. There was no decision to make. Aeron was her sister. Asked for or not, Riona was going to help her.

During the night, she'd ripped the straps

holding her arms. In the end, she'd decided the gown really was a nuisance. It didn't allow her to blend with the crowd, considering everyone she saw was in the traditional tunic attire of the Qurilixian people. As she'd made her way around the edge of the campsite, she'd received curious stares. Riona had walked with purpose, hoping if she pretended to know what she was doing no one would question her presence.

The dining platform from the night before had been dismantled, and now a low stage was in its place. A royal couple presided over the crowd in matching purple clothes in the middle of the stage. The crowns gave away their rank. Riona looked at the jewelry, wishing she was that kind of skilled thief. In the right market, she could get several thousand for them. If Aeron was right and they saved this world, maybe they could collect a reward. That would go a long way to helping her make good on her debt.

Riona took a deep breath, instantly dismissing the thought. She would not exploit tragedy. She might be many things—degenerate gambler, petty criminal, thrill seeker, bad sister, borderline pirate—but she would not seek to profit on the lives of others.

Around the king and queen, several older, very serious-looking men stood. Politicians, no doubt.

People gathered to watch, though not nearly the numbers that had been at the party the night before. She could well guess the majority of the celebrants slept off the excess drinking.

Movement in the crowd caught her attention, but it was too hard to see what was happening from her place hidden in the back. If she was going to watch for her sister, she needed a closer view of the proceedings.

MIREK SPENT THE NIGHT ALONE, overlooking the festival ground from a cliff above the low valley. Normally, his brothers would have joined him there, but they were all with new brides. Liquor and sadness made for hard company, and his sour mood did not lessen with the sunrise. Despite this, he knew his duty. Light only deepened the profound feeling of loneliness, as he faced the first dawn of his brothers' happiness.

"Many blessings, my brothers," he whispered, meaning it. His self-pity would not reach beyond this moment. He would bury the pain deep and return to work for that is all he had. Work. Duty. Work. Duty. The endless cycle felt meaningless with no wife and sons to share his life with.

After packing up the makeshift campsite, he

headed back down to the valley to watch his brothers announce their marriages. His presence in the crowd would show his support. How could the others begin to understand how hard it was for him to be there?

Climbing down the cliff was easier in shifted form. He took a deep breath, letting the tough dark brown flesh of the dragon work its way over his skin. A ridge grew from his forehead to create a protective shield over his nose and brow. Fangs extended in his mouth and talons grew from his nail bed. His body remained relatively the same shape, but he was stronger this way, tougher. In his dragon form, he could move with great agility and he didn't hesitate to jump off the side of the cliff, turning in midair to land against a rocky edge. He swung his feet back and forth like a pendulum, falling a little with each pass only to catch and release his weight with his hands. Within a few moments, he reached the bottom.

Instantly, he focused his senses to gauge his surroundings. It was an old habit, one drilled into them during their youth when training to fight. The ceremonies had started. A couple made love in the forest a few miles to the southeast. Birds sang, signifying all was well to the west. And…footsteps.

There was something off about the way the person walked. The steps were too light and measured. Mirek frowned. Could it be the Var dared to come to their festival? The enemy cat-shifting race ruled the lands to the south. King Attor would be a fool to send his soldiers so close to the Draig palace. He listened a moment longer. The steps did not sound like Var.

Curious more than concerned, he followed the sound. For the first time since the failed ceremony, his mind was distracted by something other than self-indulgent misery. His heartbeat quickened. Perhaps he was a little drunk, or overtired, or emotionally drained, but he thought to detect the faint scent of a woman on the breeze. He followed it, mindlessly needing to discover the end of this trail. All of his senses focused on the sound of those feet. His breathing deepened, not from the exertion, but from a strange sense of excitement.

"Welcome to the family of Draig, Lady Aeron. I hope you will enjoy your new home," the queen's voice announced loudly from the ceremonial stage. A bride had just been presented to the council of elders. Mirek listened past the sound as he followed his prey.

"Aeron." The word was soft, almost too soft to hear. "Aeron, what have you done?"

He concentrated on the feminine voice, finding the bearer pressed against a thick banner post. Overhead, the royal standard flapped heavily in the breeze. He narrowed his gaze, taking in every tiny detail. She wore the gown of a bride about to walk through the procession line. However, he'd seen all the women. He was sure he'd have remembered the deep reddish brown of this one's hair and the lush curve of her hips.

As if sensing his interest in it, the woman ran her hands through her hair and shook it lightly. Mirek couldn't help but smile at the way the sunlight rippled over it. Her temple hit hard against the post. He moved closer. She didn't hear his approach as she spoke to herself in the old star language. "Blast it all, Aeron. What did you do? This wasn't the plan."

Plan? The woman must have known she was fated by the gods to marry during this particular ceremony. Only, he hadn't found her. No wonder she was upset.

Mirek caught her scent—exotic and sweet but tinged with the floral perfume Galaxy Brides had provided. He breathed deeply, drawn closer still. Desire rippled through him and he had no power to control it.

As if sensing him, she glanced in his direction. The woman stiffened and gave a small gasp of surprise. Her eyes swept down the length of him. He realized he was still shifted into dragon form.

Mirek let the shift fade from his features. "Don't be frightened."

The woman remained stiff, but he didn't sense fear in her at his physical change. Quietly, she said, "Where did you come from? I didn't hear…hear…green."

Light brown eyes found his. Her mouth continued to move, but no sound escaped her as she stared at him. She was perhaps the most stunning creature he'd ever seen. How had he missed her during the ceremony? Just her nearness sparked a rock-hard interest between his thighs. No, it was more than lust. He felt her inside him. The energy between them snapped and pulled. He leaned toward her, drawn by her eyes, her scent, the pant of her breath. Her lips parted. Her eyelids fluttered.

"Really green." She reached for his face, staring at his eyes. The touch of her hand was like heaven. It warmed him and sent a chill through him at the same time.

"How did I miss you?" he wondered aloud, moving to caress her cheek as she did his.

"I don't know," she whispered, as dazed as he.

"Do you feel?" he asked.

"Yes," she sighed.

Her lips were right there, waiting. Mirek moaned softly, unmindful of where he was. He kissed her hard and she let him. The magnetic pull between them grew, crushing their bodies together. Somehow, he knew he stole her breath and he forced himself to let go. She gasped for air. Her chest heaved against him. The taste of her tongue was in his mouth. Impatient hands begged him to rip her clothing from her. He flexed his fingers.

Seeing a soft glow against her jaw, he looked at his crystal. The stone gave off a brilliant light. He'd found her. His blessing.

The sound of voices drew him back to reality—at least enough to where he could reason about what was happening. As much as he hated to, he let her go for the sake of propriety. The memory of her body against his still burned into his length.

Urgency filled him. He'd taken his mask off the night before. This was all wrong. It wasn't happening the right way. Tradition dictated they spent the night together in a tent. She was supposed to remove his mask, a symbol of her acceptance of him, and then they would talk and explore each other without consummation. In the morning, they made their commitment known by going in front of the council and crushing the crystal, thus cementing their bond. Only then could they come together in the most glorious of lustful acts.

He couldn't wait another year for her. Already

he felt as if he would explode. Surely the fact all his brothers and cousins had found mates meant this was his time as well. A lot could happen in a year. She might not want to wait for him. His body could not wait to claim her, not with the memory of her willingness and the taste of her kiss to haunt him.

"What is your name?" Mirek demanded. Desperation filled him. He had to act.

"Riona Grey."

"I will make it up to you, Riona," he whispered, "but I cannot wait a year. Surely the gods meant for me to find you this year like the others found their wives. I feel you deep in me."

She blinked, not answering. Her attention turned to the crystal and then back to his face. The glassy-eyed look meant the crystal's power was taking a fierce hold on her.

"Come," he said impatiently.

Mirek took her by the hand and led her to the stage. He didn't stop to think. How could he? He'd spent the entire night convinced he'd be forever alone. Now that he found her, he wasn't letting her go. He'd figure out the rest later.

The king was absent as Mirek led her up to the stage. He pulled his bride before his aunt. "Queen Mede, may I present my bride, Lady Riona Grey."

The queen eyed the woman's bridal attire curiously. It was not customary to wear the garments in the morning light, but neither was there a law against it. Mirek had already changed his loincloth from the night before into breeches, but he wore no shirt. Mede glanced behind her throne toward the forest, clearly looking for her husband. When his uncle the king didn't appear, she said, "Proceed."

Mirek took the crystal from his neck and pressed it into Riona's hand. "Break this."

She lifted the glowing crystal, studied it and then grabbed hold with both hands. Pressing her thumbs up, she cracked it into two. The light faded. The crowd cheered.

"Ow," Riona gasped, sticking her thumb into her mouth. Mirek detected the scent of blood. She'd cut herself. Blinking heavily, she looked at him and then the crowd. "What…? What am I doing here?"

"Welcome to the family of Draig, Lady Riona. I hope you will enjoy your new home," the queen said.

Confusion passed over Riona's face as she glanced at the queen and then Mirek. "But…?"

The queen stood from her throne and came to Mirek. Placing a hand on her nephew's arm, she squeezed it tight. There was no other indication that she was displeased as she smiled brightly at them. Under her breath, she ordered, "Mirek, there is a reason we send fresh clothing to the tents.

You may enjoy your bride in such a state, but stop whatever game you play and give her the tunic dress." She eyed his clothing dispassionately. "And change into your formal attire as well. You look as if you're about to run straight home dragging this poor woman behind you. I expected better of you, Ambassador."

Mirek nodded, unable to help his grin of excitement. "Yes, my queen. She may have whatever she wishes."

"Good. See to it. If I get a report that you are not treating her properly, I will not be pleased." The queen let go and moved to take her seat just as the king reappeared. The royal couple spoke in low tones as the queen explained what had happened in his absence.

"What am I doing on stage?" Riona whispered. A tiny trail of blood ran down her uplifted finger, but she didn't seem to notice it.

Mirek took her by the arm and led her quickly from the onlookers. "Don't worry. It's done. We're all right. The blessing has been received."

"What's done?" she asked, as he pulled her past the crowd toward the tents. "Blessing?"

"They didn't suspect," he said. "We're all right."

Riona jerked her arm from him, refusing to

walk farther. "Who are you, crazy man? What is all right?"

"Lord Miroslav, Ealdorman of Draig," Mirek answered. Joy like he'd never known exploded within him, filling his heart. Nothing could take away his happiness. Nothing. "You may call me Mirek. I am your husband. We are wed."

I AM YOUR HUSBAND. We are wed.

Riona stared at the disconcerting man before her. Surely that is not what she'd heard. Her mind felt a little fuzzy, like when she'd spent three days drinking after an intergalactic tournament. She had the strangest impression that she'd kissed this man and thoroughly enjoyed doing it, but that was impossible. She didn't kiss strangers—no matter how drunk she was or how sexy they were.

"What just happened?" she asked. "One moment I'm watching my sister make a really stupid mistake, and the next I'm the one on stage with a cut finger and people are cheering. What in all the bounty of Jareth is going on here?"

"I do not know this Jareth."

"It's just an old saying. Where's my sister?" she demanded. "I have to find my sister. Some guy was trying to make her a bride."

"If she is here, we will find her." The Mirek guy was smiling at her. She inched away from him, a little worried about his sanity. He continued, "This is truly a blessed day. Your sister is married. My brothers and cousins are married. I am sure you will see her very soon, and you must invite her to our castle home in the mountains."

Did crazy half-naked dragon man just say he wanted to take her away to the mountains? Her parents might have exploded, but Riona was pretty sure there had been a childhood lesson warning her against traveling to secluded places with irrational strangers.

"You were not frightened by my shift." His words were more of a statement than a question.

"No. Should I be?" She glanced around, unconcerned that the planet was filled with shape-shifters. In their modern society, everyone was an alien. She was an alien. For all he knew, she grew fangs and spat poison. She didn't, but that would have been a useful trick.

"They took the extra tents down," he said, drawing her attention back to him. "But I will find a place where we can get out of these clothes and into proper attire."

Riona looked down at the ridiculous dress she still wore and ignored the tiny thrill of pleasure his statement caused. She licked her lips, feeling as if a strange pressure was against them. "You are not getting me out of these clothes."

"You wish to keep the dress? There is no law against it. You may treasure the gown forever, my bride, whatever you wish." He still smiled at her.

Blast it all, but he was a handsome man. And his eyes, so green they reminded her of… Well, in truth they didn't remind her of anything. In all her travels, she'd never seen eyes so captivating, and looking directly into them made it hard to breathe.

"I will keep the loincloth as well," he stated, seeming very eager to please. "I have it at my campsite if you wish to see it later."

Riona almost said yes to that. She pursed her lips tightly together and clenched her teeth to keep the word inside. When did the planet surface temperature become so hot? Her body heat spiked. And tingly. When did the planet become so tingly?

"I don't understand that expression," he admitted. "You wish to see it now?"

Yes, please. Now, please.

"Uh, you know what I could really use…Lord Mirek, was it?" Riona gave him her sweetest, most alluring smile. She needed to put distance between them. "I could use a drink. A really strong one. It's been a pretty long night."

"Long night? Yes, I am sorry I did not find you in the receiving line, my lady. It was a very long night for me as well." His smile dropped by small degrees. "But we will be happy. I promise I will do everything to make you happy."

"I could use a drink," she repeated, not knowing what else to say. "That will make me happy."

"Drink?" He nodded, grinning wider as if she'd just bestowed the greatest favor on him. "I can find that." He looked around before leading her behind a tent. "Wait here."

Riona watched the man hurry away from her. Okay, so he was really handsome in a crazy I-just-tried-to-marry-a-stranger-and-asked-her-to-go-into-the-secluded-mountains-with-me sort of way. When he was out of sight, she turned back toward the stage. She didn't have time to deal with the lunatic calling himself her husband. For the most part, he seemed harmless enough, not aggressive, just overly certain of their life together.

Riona needed to find Aeron before this Bron Duke person decided he wanted to drag her sister off into the mountains. If her sister left the area, Riona would have a hard time trying to track her over alien territory. Ship signatures, she could follow. Ground prints, not so well.

Riona made her way across the encampment to where she'd last seen Aeron being led away by her husband—actually, *captor* had a nicer ring to it—being led away by her captor.

Going into an alien forest wasn't her crowning adventure, but she also wasn't adverse to a little danger. Like before, she walked as if she had purpose, making her way across the landscape of ashen bonfire pits. A few of them still had red embers burning inside them. Giant logs surrounded the pits and large footprints littered the dirt. Empty wine goblets were left on the ground with a few stray pieces of clothing. The party had apparently gotten pretty wild the night before. Riona had heard the celebration, but she'd been too busy watching the Galaxy Brides ship for her sister.

A loud scream followed by rolling laughter drew her attention to the ceremonial grounds. A man in a loincloth marched across the campground with a fully clothed woman over his shoulder. Blonde hair flew about her head, the shade of it giving the woman's identity away. She was Pia, perhaps the most gorgeous woman on the Galaxy Brides ship, if not one of the quieter ones. Riona felt sorry for the woman. No one deserved to be treated like that—especially not by a husband. However, Pia, like the rest of the brides, had chosen her fate, and there was no point in Riona's interfering. She had her own sister to worry about. Moreover, if her estimation was correct, she'd lay high odds on the fact Pia could well handle herself in this situation. The warrior man carrying Pia off might be large, but size didn't always matter. The woman moved with the grace of a fighter.

Riona kept going. The giant trees of the forest made it hard to see within the depths. She was forced to walk around one large trunk and then another. Almost instantly, the campsite disappeared from view behind a wall of bark even though she could hear the low hum of conversation punctuated by random bursts of laughter. She dropped all pretense of blending in and ran toward the back of the stage where she'd last seen her sister. The speed was reckless, but she couldn't waste any more time. Aeron's trail might go cold. First, she needed to find her sister. Second, she needed to find a ship to steal.

The ground changed. She ran onto a steep incline, grabbing hold of a tree limb when the sheer willpower of her legs couldn't make the trip up and over the edge.

"This was not well done of us, bride," a man said as Riona crawled onto a cushion of yellow plants. The words caused her to press low to the ground. She found the bearer of the voice easily. Bron carried her sister in his arms. Aeron wasn't moving. Her limbs flailed uselessly as he turned her. "You will understand, woman, that you are my wife. You will not leave me. I cannot let you go. Once we're in the mountain fortress, you—"

Riona gave a soft gasp of alarm. The man glanced around the forest. She buried her face in the yellow groundcover and closed her eyes tight, careful not to move.

4

DRAIG NORTHERN MOUNTAIN FORTRESS, PLANET OF QURILIXEN

Aeron?

Riona tried to lift her head. It felt heavy, as if a weight pressed down upon her skull. She flung her hand over her face, swatting at the air. Nothing was there. Her vision was blurred, light and shadows dancing in chaos.

What happened? Where was she?

She swung her arm again. It was the only limb that worked. A strange, dull lethargy vibrated along her nerves. This wasn't right. She shouldn't feel like this. Her legs were there, she felt them, but they were paralyzed. Her feet itched but she couldn't scratch one foot with the other's toenails.

What's happening?

Aeron?

Thinking of her sister, Riona forced her unwilling body to move. She felt the cold press of metal against her hand and grabbed it. With a groan, she pulled. Her body slid a few inches. Unfortunately, the act used up her reserve of strength and her arm fell, shaking and useless.

"Stop moving," she whispered to her vision. The dancing lights and shadows did not listen. She closed her eyes. It helped a little, but then her mind began to spin, making her nauseous. A tear slid over her cheek. What was happening to her?

The numbness began to burn. Every nerve lit with instant heat. And still she couldn't move her limbs. She was trapped in the ever-growing blaze of invisible fire.

A scream ripped from her throat. The sound didn't help, but it was the only thing she could manage.

MIREK JERKED awake and leapt out of bed. He was completely shifted into dragon form by the time his feet hit the ground. He followed the sound of the scream, ignoring the stone steps leading down to the main level of his home as he jumped over the curving metal rail to land on the floor below. His shifted legs absorbed the fall easily. He kept running. Riona's screams only grew louder.

At the far end of his home, he slid to a stop and pressed his taloned fingers into the door sensor. It scanned his biometric signature. The privacy setting was activated on the door so he couldn't see inside. He kept it that way to give his wife privacy when visitors came to his home. The screams blasted now that the isolation room was opened.

"Riona," Mirek said, hurrying inside. He knew she wouldn't hear him. She never had in all the months she'd been in the isolation room he'd built for her. Still, he kept talking. "It will be over in a moment."

He grabbed the hand-held medic unit and went to her side. The sight of her red skin blistered and peeling still alarmed him every time he saw it. The Medical Alliance doctors had likened it to being thrown into a fire that never completely snuffed.

He'd only spoken to his wife while she was conscious for a short time at their wedding ceremony, but he could well remember what she looked like without the wounds. When he closed his eyes, the rush he felt upon first seeing her, his life mate, came over him anew. He tried to hold on to that moment, those few words spoken. It was hard in light of her screaming in agony.

Mirek held the unit against her arm and

pressed a button. Medicine was injected into her. The screams fell into moans filled with pain. The medicine was working. He couldn't touch her, couldn't hold her. If he tried to physically comfort her it would only hurt her more. Helpless, all he could do was wait and pray to his gods that her illness would end soon, or that he may take it from her. Mirek would give anything to take her place so her suffering would stop. Months might have passed, but it felt like a lifetime. At first, she'd been deathlike, a limp doll in his arms. Then the screaming had started. It was becoming worse and there was nothing he could do to stop it.

He stood over her, watching until she settled into a dreamless sleep. Taking her arm that had fallen aside, he gingerly lifted it and placed it next to her. His touch made her groan in protest. Her position on the bed was off center, but he decided not to try to move her.

When the moans finally stopped, he hoped she couldn't feel what was happening to her. He had a lot of time to think about it and knew this punishment should have been his. He was the one who'd defied the gods and taken her before the council so that they may marry without spending the traditional night in the marriage tent. It was his haste to be married, his vanity and pride, that had brought this upon her. What other explanation was there?

He should have waited a year for the next ceremony. The gods had revealed her after the ceremony, they'd wanted to give him hope for the coming year, but he'd failed their test and claimed her early. This was a steep price to pay for his impatience.

"I'm sorry, Riona," he whispered, sinking to the floor. The cold metal of the isolation room stung his naked flesh, but he didn't care. Why should he be comfortable when his wife was in so much pain? "This is not how it should be."

Mirek remained well past the moment the cold chilled his flesh and the hard floor caused his body to ache. He wanted to suffer. He deserved to suffer. Yet for all the physical discomfort, the worst part was watching his sick, unmoving bride. He stared at her chest, counting her breaths, desperate for the moment her anguish would end.

WATCHING Lady Clara of the Redding reunite with her parents was painfully awkward to behold. The visiting nobleman, the Great Lord of the Redding, demanded the customary pleasantries—not that there was much pleasantness to the great lord. In fact, the man was as emotionless as his daughter had been when she'd first arrived at the Breeding

Festival. Mirek had almost rather invited the Lithorians over for drinks and stare sideways for an hour while reciting the proper talking phrases. At least at the end of that meeting the women would have their chocolate.

Then again, Great Lord of the Redding was assisting them with ridding Qurilixen's mines of an alien menace. The Tyoe aliens had tried to take over their ore mines and had pumped nasty chemicals into their mountains to do it. Clara's species of humanoid had telepathic powers that interfered with the Tyoe's biochemistry, basically boiling them from the inside without having to touch them. Needless to say, the Tyoe did not want to fight the Redde armies in battle and had flown away as fast as their gelatinous little bodies could take them.

Mirek reminded himself to be a little more understanding of the Redde's stoic ways. And technically, these people were family since Lady Clara had married Mirek's brother, Vlad. Even now, after she'd settled into her marriage, it was hard to determine what Clara was thinking. He'd give her credit for trying to smile, but sometimes the gesture seemed forced, giving credence to the fact she'd not been allowed to show her emotions growing up.

Despite her limitations when it came to facial expressions, Clara was a very caring person. She visited Riona every day, even though the sleeping lady was a stranger to her. That alone gave Mirek a high opinion of his new sister. So when she'd asked him to greet her parents, he'd agreed without question.

They were in the scroll room, one of the few rooms in the fortress home that the visitors deemed suitable to their nobility. Mirek suspected it had to do more with the comfort of the wide chairs to accommodate the great lady's large clothing than anything else. Mirek watched as Clara lifted her hand and let her wrist hover before her mother's painted face. Their towering wigs had amused him at first. He remembered thinking his nephews might have cone-shaped heads.

Great Lady Jaene's dress must have weighed more than her spaceship. It was constructed with more jewels than material. The heavy stones formed a giant fat bell of a skirt and glistened in the light when she moved. It was the same type of dress Clara had donned at her wedding. Now Clara wore a shapeless bag of pink and purple stripes over her frame, which she referred to as a traditional Redde maternity gown, due to her advancing pregnancy. Otherwise pregnant-shaped daughter bell would probably fall over trying to lift her hand forward to greet mother bell. Both women's faces were pale from white paint with bright spots of color to accent the cheeks, lashes and lips.

Clara did not dress like a Redde noblewoman when her parents were gone. In fact, Mirek thought her much happier when her parents were away. Or rather, she looked happier.

"Welcome to my home, Great Lady," Clara said solemnly to her mother, not showing any emotion in her expression. The Redde people did not do anything warmly.

Jaene lifted her hand to greet her daughter, holding her wrist out to hover before Clara's face before letting it fall. They didn't touch. In a whisper Mirek could easily hear, the visiting lady said, "I am glad to see the barbarians let you have your cosmetics."

"I had them on last time you visited," Clara reminded her.

"But not the first time. I still dream ill from seeing your naked flesh." Jaene gave a sidelong glance to Mirek. This was the third time Great Lord and Lady had deigned to visit their daughter's new home world. If there was affection in the family, Mirek couldn't see it. Great Lord acted more concerned with his powdered wig and long jacket remaining immaculate than his daughter's new life. Being a Redde male, he did not wear the cosmetics.

Clara also looked at Mirek briefly before gesturing to her gown to redirect the conversation,

"I received your noble maternity package. Thank you, Great Lady."

They kept speaking, but Mirek didn't really listen. He tugged at his sleeve to reveal the thin white band around his wrist, taking comfort in seeing it was there. He hadn't wanted to leave his wife, but after months of pacing his home waiting for her to wake up, he didn't have much of a choice. He had duties to attend to. As the Mining Ambassador, he couldn't keep putting off his responsibilities. He was, quite literally, his people's link to the outside worlds, and it fell to him to deal with any visiting aliens. Normally, he enjoyed his work.

The band on his arm began to tickle. He dug a finger under it and scratched. When the bracelet vibrated it indicated movement inside his wife's isolation chamber. Itching probably meant he needed to charge the device or the sensor was broken. When he'd checked on her that morning, nothing had changed, and her bouts with pain only seemed to happen during the night hours. He shook his wrist several times to get it to stop.

Lady Jaene moved her hovering wrist to Clara's stomach. Her eyes darkened slightly. "Your grandson does very well, Great Lord." This seemed to please the man, who nodded a couple of times. Clara's mother wasn't the only one with special sensing abilities. The Redde women communicated with things most people could not. Clara, herself, carried a telepathic link to the ceffyl herds. Mirek rarely rode the creatures, but many of his people did. He spent most of his time on space ships.

"How is the next generation?" Clara asked. "And my siblings? Are my sisters adjusting well after their pregnancy stasis?"

"Thirty girls," Great Lord stated, as if that was answer enough.

"They are very happy you finally married so that your sisters were allowed to wake up and start their families," Jaene said. "Great Lord was perceptive in his resolve to send you here. Your son is proof that he is very wise in his decisions and should not be questioned."

Did Jaene just give credit to her husband for the Qurilixen blue sun's genetic-altering properties?

Mirek absently scratched at the band. The tickling sensation grew worse and he stiffened, making a small sound of realization.

"Lord Mirek?" Clara asked, her eyes rounding slightly. She looked from his face to his wrist? A ghost of a smile began to play over her features but she quickly subdued it. "Your presence is not required at this time. I wish to hear about my nieces. Please rejoin us when it is convenient for you to do so."

He nodded his thanks as she gave him an out. Mumbling what he hoped was the proper phrases, he walked quickly from the room. The vibration against his flesh grew. Mirek forced himself to keep walking until he reached the end of the commons area. Clara's parents would be insulted if he ran.

Alek stood with his wife, a very pregnant Kendall, in the corridor joining Mirek's home to his brothers'. Her cheeks were flushed from their daily walk around the forest. When Alek tried to smile at him, Mirek simply shot past, turning the corner to run down the hall leading to his private wing.

"Mirek? What is it?" Kendall called after him. "Do you need help?"

"My wife," Mirek yelled in excitement and fear. The vibrations grew more insistent and the fierceness of its silent alarm could only mean one thing. "My wife is finally awake!"

"Aw-ow!" Riona groaned as she pushed up. The medical unit she lay on retracted its needle. The sharp, fat point alone looked bigger than some of the knives she'd carried in her travels. Automatically reaching for her back to feel where it had been inserted, she winced. Her fingers came back smeared with blood and a sticky green substance. Whatever it had been doing to her, it hadn't finished the job.

Beneath the smear of blood on her fingers, her skin was red and bumpy. Tiny blisters ran their way up her forearm covered in a fine white powder. She examined her skin, flipping her hand back and forth, as if staring would make the blemishes go away. Riona slapped at her arm, trying to wipe the blisters off, only to realize her other arm looked just as bad. She was covered.

Touching her face, she searched for a reflective surface. The best she could find was the thick door. It would have been clear but for the privacy setting obscuring the outside from view. She made a move to stand only to feel a tug at her waist. She lifted her arms, recoiling from the sight of thick yellow tubes inserted into her side. Shaking, she pulled at them, wanting them out. The medical tubes must have been inside her for a while because the friction of removing them burned, indicating her body had begun to heal itself to them. She gave a small cry as they finally tugged free. Yellow fluid tinged with blood trickled from the wounds.

The small room was built as some sort of laboratory. Hand-held medics, injector refills and other more primitive medicines lined the transparent cabinet on the wall. She walked past the bottles, seeing tight handwritten script on the apothecary containers. The air smelled sickeningly sweet, like a decontaminator after its cleaning cycle. The only real furniture was the medical bed she'd been resting on.

Holding her side, she limped to the door to see her face. A drop of blood trickled down her back and trailed over her naked skin. Her blurred reflection revealed red splotches along her entire body—her *very naked* body. She belatedly covered her chest with a gasp and looked for her clothes. It didn't take long to deduce there was nothing for her to wear.

Frightened, she went to the door sensor and placed her hand against it. The unit tried to suck her finger into the wall. She jerked back just in time to see an electrical snap inside the formed indent where her finger had been. The sensor molded back into a flat surface.

Drawing attention to her naked self was the last thing she wanted to do, but what choice did she have? It was quite possible sensors had detected her movements the second she'd awoken and alerted her captors.

The room looked a little too technically advanced for the primitive Draig people. Had they sold her? Or worse, had Range found her? She remembered intense agony and being paralyzed. It would be like him to take out his frustrations in such a way. She looked at her skin. Well, she wouldn't have taken him for being *this* sadistic, but then she'd never skipped out on owing him fifty-thousand space credits before.

Who was she trying to fool? The money would be secondary to the man's pride. Insulting the pirate didn't seem as funny at the moment. The thing about criminals was they didn't have a problem breaking the law. Kidnapping, torture... Riona looked at her hips and legs. What else had they done to her? Her lower stomach hurt, but then so did the rest of her body.

"Hello?" Her voice was raspy and her throat ached.

Riona couldn't think about it. If he'd sexually assaulted her, that very act would have begun her biological countdown.

"Range?" she called, leaning her forehead against the door. There was no one else angry enough with her to do this. The only way she would have such a rash was if it was intentional. It wasn't like they were living in the twentieth century. Medical booths could cure just about anything. If someone had enough technology to put her in this room, they could have easily given her medical treatment. The fact her skin was flaking off in strange patches meant her current state was on purpose. "I know you can hear me. You've had your fun. Now it's time to deal."

He didn't answer.

"You have to listen, Range. Think about your crew. What's more important? Revenge or loot? I can get your money for you. In fact, I was working on it when you came for me. That little planet you picked me up on, you saw it, you know the kind of primitives they have there. Well, they also have an ore that's worth a fortune."

Still, no answer.

"I was going to get you jewels," she whispered, thinking of the royal crowns. She should have taken them. At the time, she hadn't wanted to be that kind of thief, but in light of her painfully real alternative, she was quickly changing her mind. Tears threatened her eyes and she hated the weakness of them. Her voice barely sounded as she added, "I had a way to get a reward. I was going to save them from…"

Still, nothing.

She hit her hand hard against the door. "Blast it, Range! Let me out of here. I told you I can get you your money. All I need is a little bit of time. I had the angle all worked out." She thought of the crazy man who called her his wife. No part of her liked what she was doing, but she had little choice. If not only to save herself, Riona thought of her sister. Aeron would not last in such a primitive place. Her sister wasn't built for adventure. She'd seen the Galaxy Brides ship leave. She'd seen that possessive man carry Aeron off. "Range, I have a mark. He doesn't suspect a thing. In fact, he thinks I'm marrying him. I'll have your credits for you in no time."

The longer silence persisted, the more worried she became. There was no telling where she was. The room was small. Surely that meant she was on a ship somewhere. When she closed her eyes, she felt the room move and her weak body sway. Those tiny vibrations could only mean one thing. Turbulent space travel. Right?

"Range?" Her voice lost some of its bravado. Tired, she leaned into the door, pressing her forehead against her wrist. "By the bounty of Jareth, I swear this guy is an easy mark. I'll have enough *Galaxa-promethium* to pay you back twice over. *Galaxa-promethium*, Range, that's the ore for long-distance space travel. It's like liquid currency. Everyone will accept it. Now let me out of here so we can negotiate the interest rate…"

Riona's words trailed off as she detected movement. Feet were outside the door. She lifted her head as it slid open to keep from falling.

"It's about time," she said with a boldness she didn't feel. "Now how about giving a girl some…"

It wasn't Range. Her heart nearly stopped in her chest. The half-naked *husband* from the Breeding Festival stood before her. He was the very last person she expected to see.

"Clothes," she finished weakly. "You're not…"

"Range?" the man supplied coldly.

"Naked," she whispered, confused.

Though he was fully dressed, she remembered what he'd looked like in a pair of snug pants at the festival grounds. He'd been bare-chested then. Now, he wore an immaculately tailored, loose-fitting shirt that hung over his tight pants. A tiny, symmetrical pattern had been embroidered around the bottom hem of the shirt. It was vastly different than the savage garb of the wedding event. Like this, he appeared refined. How was it she'd dismissed him as some crazy barbarian before?

Confused, she glanced behind him. It wasn't a ship. In fact, it appeared as if she was in someone's home. This man's most likely. The place was lavish, all smooth stone walls and floors with thick rugs and wooden furniture. The oversized décor fit nicely into the spacious abode. A banner of a dragon standard hung on the wall. Its predominant placement gave away its importance. When she again looked at him, she saw his eyes shift and change with a golden hue. She knew the Draig men were dragon-shifters. She'd seen him turn. The fact he had special abilities hardly scared her. She'd seen plenty of aliens, even if this one happened to be an incredibly sexy-crazy alien who made her heart beat a little faster. Already weak from whatever strange illness plagued her skin, she swayed on her feet but managed to keep standing.

"Are you in pain?" he asked.

She shook her head in denial. It was a lie. She hurt, but that was secondary at the moment.

"Princess Nadja sent some medicines for you to try once you awoke to help with any pain should you start feeling it," he said.

"Nadja from the ship? She's a princess?" Riona recalled the quiet, dignified woman. That made sense. Nadja was very poised as if she came from money and privilege. "Why would she care about my pain?"

"She's your cousin-by-marriage and wants to help," the dragon man stated. "She's been studying plant properties on the planet."

He made a move as if to touch her face and she flinched, snapping her head away.

"Where is this place?" she whispered. Nothing about it made sense. The Draig were primitive people. This was not a primitive home. "It doesn't look like your planet."

"This is our planet and this is your new home, wife," the man ground out between his teeth. She felt more than saw the irritation in him. It radiated off every rigid gesture, seeping from his pores. Guilt compounded fear. She stepped back, very aware of how vulnerable she was in her naked state. The room was small, too small. She didn't answer. How could she? He stared at her for a long moment and then added, "I hope it's not too primitive for you."

With that, he turned and left her.

Riona instantly regretted the insult meant for Range's ears. She'd never have said it to this man's face. Insulting innocent people was not her style. She knew in that second, his parting look would be one of those rare moments forever emblazoned in her memory. She didn't know him well enough to read the expression, but the look of it would haunt her as she forever tried to decipher what it had meant.

He left the door open, not trapping her inside. She didn't follow him, not right away. Instead, she stood looking out into the wealthy home he'd invited her into. There was nothing primitive about it. She had been so sure she was on Range's ship. A strange sense of relief and worry filled her. At least with Range, she knew what she was up against. He would act in the interest of himself and his crew. This man, this *husband*, was a mystery.

A mystery she was stuck with.

Riona looked down at her side. The bleeding hadn't stopped. She swayed on her feet and pressed her hand to the wound. Maybe forcibly yanking medical tubes out of her body hadn't been the best way to remove them.

"Ah, dragon guy?" she whispered as she lifted her bloody hand to look at it. "I hate to trouble you, but..." She half-sank, half-fell to the floor. Riona pressed her head to the door frame and closed her eyes. "I'm not doing so well."

Mirek's heart pounded, but he wasn't sure if it was excitement, or fear, or anger that caused the violent reaction in his chest. Her words stung. In his happiness to see her awake, he was tempted to forget what she'd said. But that would be foolish, wouldn't it? Her motives for marrying him were in those words.

Mirek wasn't like his brothers and cousins. He had an intuitive knowledge from his exposure to other alien cultures. The rest of the universe did not think as they did. It was possible that his bride did not marry for love or for fate. It could be as she'd said, she'd married him for money.

His heart argued that it was the will of the

gods. His crystal had glowed. This was fate. The gods had brought her to him.

His mind countered that no one really knew why the crystal glowed. It could be fate or it could be the combination of sex pheromones and lack of radiation from the sun at night. He'd had the thought before but had never let himself actually consider it as a possibility. Mirek wanted so much to believe in fate.

He had to believe in something. He had to believe in the will of the gods. If there wasn't fate, then what was there? And if he had doubts, would the gods continue to punish him and force her back to sleep?

This was a test. The gods had made her say those things and they watched to see if he was worthy.

Curses! He was going to fail.

He couldn't fail.

But what if he did? His wife didn't deserve such punishment.

And yet…

"Mirek? Is it true?"

He blinked, looking up in surprise to see Aeron waddling toward him. She was adorably pregnant like the rest of his sisters-by-marriage.

"Is my sister awake?" Aeron asked. Her features were flushed and she was lady enough not to mention the fact she'd caught him arguing with himself.

"Yes. I was coming to tell you. She's awake. She's…"

Aeron frowned in worry. She grabbed his arm. "What it is? Is it bad? I can tell by your face something is not as it should be."

"She's awake. Her medical readings look good from what I can tell, but she doesn't want me touching her. I thought maybe she'd let you examine her, seeing as you're familiar to her?"

"Familiar?" Aeron gave a soft laugh. The sound was filled with happiness and relief. She walked Mirek back toward his home.

"She does not know me," Mirek stated, tortured by the truth in his words.

"You said she was awake when you claimed her. Is her memory suffering?" Aeron asked.

"She should know me regardless," he said. "Just as you would know Bron if you were to lose your memories. It is inside you."

"That connection took time," she assured him. "Can I assume by your expression that my sister was her normally charming self?" Aeron squeezed his arm. "If she insulted you, that's probably a good sign that she's functioning like normal."

He frowned.

"Whatever Riona said or did, Mirek, you have

to forgive her. My sister has many blocks inside her, just as I did when I first arrived. Give her time. She doesn't know everything you have done. She doesn't know what you've been through for her." Aeron gave a long sigh and touched her stomach. "Your nephew does like to kick me."

Mirek automatically reached to feel the baby. A tiny thump resounded against his hand and he smiled. "He is strong."

"What did she say to you?"

"She thought I was someone named Range." He hoped Aeron would fill him in.

"Range? I almost forgot about him. She has been asleep a long time, hasn't she?" At his expectant look, Aeron added, "I'm sure she'll tell you about it. I honestly don't know much about her life."

Mirek didn't press the issue as he opened the door to his home.

"Ri?" Aeron called, hurrying past him to see her sister. She came to a sudden stop. "Mirek, help!"

Mirek ran toward the isolation chamber. Riona had passed out on the floor. He shifted partially, detecting her heartbeat and breathing. "She lives. She was standing and glaring at me when I came for you."

"Stupid woman," Aeron scolded, more to

herself, as Mirek lifted Riona from the ground. "It looks like she pulled her medical tubes out. At least her skin looks much better and she doesn't scream when you touch her. Lay her down. Let's heal the wounds and I'll get her cleaned up. If the machine medically clears her we'll move her to your bed."

Mirek said nothing, merely obeyed.

5

A DREAM. It was all a dream.

Riona gasped as she struggled to sit up on the bed. She breathed heavily, feeling her sides and back for tubes and needles. Satisfied that all was well, she gave a small laugh of relief. It was all a horrible dream.

The laugh faded. Then where was she? The dark room gave hints in its shadows, but she didn't recognize her surroundings. Galaxy Brides' ship? No. This room was too large, even for a luxury craft.

When she tried to stand, she flinched in pain. Riona held her sore side. Now upright, her weak muscles protested, but she refused to lie back down.

It wasn't a dream. This was reality.

Following a tiny thread of light, she found herself in a large wardrobe. Clothes were neatly stacked on shelves and hung from hooks along one side of the wall. Boots lined a special rack. A large trunk rested in the corner. The costumes seemed a strange blend of alien cultures and did not belong together in one collection. A stack of tunic shirts hardly matched the Azoomian man-dress or the Frer short coat.

On the other side of the closet, the strappy Qurilixen bridal gown hung next to several dresses. She wasn't really a dress kind of girl, but the long male tunics were too big for her and would look like dresses if she took one of those instead. Finding a green gown with the least amount of frills and material, she then slipped it over her naked body. It was a perfect fit, even if it was floor length and looked better suited to a nunnery compound. Perhaps that was for the best. It hid the worst of her splotches. Then she eyed the male pants. Riona pulled the dress off and dropped it on the floor. So the pants were a little too big, but the loose fit was easily fixed as she wrapped the attached belt straps around her waist a couple of times. The Frer short coat worked as a shirt. It was a large square of dark green and purple swirls. She slipped it over her arms before buttoning the sides from hip to armpit. The boots on the rack next to the gowns felt as if they'd been made for her feet. She tucked the end of the baggy white pants into them to keep the hems from dragging on the floor.

Riona didn't care what she looked like at the moment. It wasn't like she was trying to win any fashionship shows. In truth, if she could keep her body upright, she'd call that a crowning win.

She limped toward the bedroom only to stop and guiltily stumble back to pick up the dress she'd dropped on the floor. Riona placed the gown on the rack where she'd found it.

Seeing a knob on the wall, she turned it. Movement overhead let more light into the bedroom. Riona noted that only one side of the giant bed had been slept in. She'd been alone. A brief wave of relief washed over her. She didn't get the rapist vibe off her would-be husband, actually far from it, so she was relatively certain her biological clock had not started its fatal countdown. Whatever was wrong with her, she would live through it.

Her body ached, but she ignored it. She searched her mind, but the details of what had happened to her weren't there. She remembered crazy, half-naked dragon man trying to marry her. She remembered cutting herself. There was a queen and smiling people and then…

"Aeron," Riona whispered. She closed her eyes, concentrating. One of the dragons had claimed her sister. On stage, they had called the man something? A something duke. The duke was taking her sister to a home in the mountains. She opened her eyes, setting her purpose. "I have to find a duke in the mountains."

It wasn't much of a plan, but it was all she had.

Riona might not be the best sister in all the known universes, might not see her sibling for years at a time, might not even know how to talk to Aeron without baiting the woman into a fight, but Riona loved her sister. In the end, Aeron was the only family she had. Normally, her sister was safe on a floating Federation base. No one would dare attack a Federation ship, and not many people would have reason to attack a boring ship full of civilian-contracted analysts. Aeron should have just called her to deal with this. Riona was better equipped to handle tough situations. She liked the idea of Aeron tucked away and protected. Federation ships were the safest places to be.

A pain ran up her right leg with every step, but she ignored it. Stairs led down to the lavish home she'd seen through the isolation chamber's door. At the time, she'd been too scared and weak to really look at it. The mausolean stone walls and floor would have made the room uncomfortable if not for the touches of fur rugs and oversized wooden furniture. A giant dragon standard stared down at her, the embroidered eyes seeming to follow her as she made her way slowly into the spacious room. The isolation chamber door was closed but the privacy shield wasn't activated. She saw a woman on her hands and knees scrubbing the floor where Riona had bled on it.

Not wanting to be detected, she slipped as quietly and quickly as she could out of the woman's line of sight. Instinctively, she went to the large wood door. Its carved panels set it apart from others in the home. As she neared, she glanced behind to make sure the servant didn't come out of the room before lifting her hand to where scanners were usually placed. She swept her fingers along the door frame. It slid open, letting her out. Riona peeked into a stone corridor. Seeing it was empty, she didn't hesitate as she left the dragon man's home.

She half-expected someone to stop her as she hobbled as fast as she could through the twists and turns of the hallway. She kept a steady course, not turning down the side corridors unless she had to. If she became lost, she needed to find her way back to the start again. Tears threatened the longer she walked, but she limped on.

"Aeron," she whispered. "I have to find Aeron."

"ALIEN!"

"Kill it, Trant, kill it!"

"Slay the creature. It wants our mines!"

Mirek suppressed a smile as the childish shouts and cheers resonated from outside. Being from Mining Village, the boys were well aware of the now-legendary fight between the invading Tyoe alien and Lady Clara. The woman had been trapped in the mines for days with her husband, Vlad. In that time, Clara had scared off the alien invader, saved the miners with them and became an instant heroine of the mines. Thinking of the very prim and proper lady speaking to her stoic parents, Mirek had to laugh.

Cenek, local caretaker to the ceffyl herd, had let the boys camp in the stables with one of the beasts who'd lost her baby around the time of the Breeding Festival. Since then, the beast had adopted them as replacement babies. This became a badge of honor when the boys discovered the heroine of the mines had a unique connection to and could communicate with the ceffyls. Unwilling to give up such a distinction, they made a point of coming back to the fortress home often to secure their place as adopted beasts. Their shouts had become a constant backdrop to the home. He quite enjoyed the noise.

Mirek turned the corner, intent on going home to check on his bride. He found it difficult to concentrate when he knew she had finally awoken from her coma. Well, briefly anyway. At least now she slept in their bed and no longer required the isolation chamber.

There was a lot he wanted to know, about her, from her…like why his wife had tried to negotiate with someone named Range by promising to use him and his *primitive* planet for their ore. The thought caused him to frown.

"Ah," a female screamed, "Stop!"

Mirek paused. There were no female children here. Instantly, he sprang into action, shifting on instinct to join whatever was happening outside his home.

"She'll suck you into her stomach, Trant," a boy warned. "That's what they do. She'll wrap her skin suit around you and suffocate you."

"Throw it!" another yelled.

"Throw it, Trant!" a young voice added. "Before it kills you!"

"Throw it! Throw it!" the chanting started.

Mirek ran out of the fortress. The boys had gathered before the front opening carved into the mountain's base. He smelled their aggression tinged with panic. Trant, one of the oldest, rushed forward in his shifted form and hefted a large stone to Mirek's right.

"They're our mines," one boy shouted.

"We're not scared of you, Tyoe," another added.

The female screamed and he turned just in time to see the stone *thunk* Riona on the side of her head. The boys cheered in excitement at their bravery.

"Riona!" Mirek growled, the word barely discernible in his dragon's voice. The boys instantly silenced. He darted forward to catch his wife as she fell. Blood ran over her temple. Her eyelids fluttered briefly before closing.

"No. What did you do?"

"My lord?" one of the boys asked, the sound soft and timid. "Did we get it?"

Mirek cradled Riona to his chest. In the brighter daylight, her skin took on a sickly green color with patches of ugly red. The blisters had lessened but the tiny bumps still marred half her face and neck, her hands and arms. Her hair had dried as she'd slept and now stood on end. Her physical appearance, coupled with the fact she wore a kind of alien garb the boys would never have had the occasion to see, made their mistake understandable.

"We finished off the alien, didn't we?" another added. "She was attacking the fortress. We saw her wounded from battle within. Do you need us to fight, my lord? We are ready to defend your family."

Mirek tried to relax. The boys' words would have been endearing if not for the fact they just tried to kill his wife. He concentrated on Riona. She breathed. Her skin was warm.

"What is the commotion?" Cenek came from inside the ceffyl stables. His voice naturally gruff, he scolded, "I thought you were going to help me."

"Cenek," Mirek let his body shift back to human form. He cradled Riona.

"What happened?" Cenek advanced through the now-worried boys.

"We thought she was an alien attacking. We know the ships come in here," Trant answered. "We're defending our homes."

"Trant threw it, not us," a young boy tattled.

"Quiet," Trant warned, balling his fists. "You told me to because you were too scared to do it yourself, coward."

"Cenek," Mirek repeated, louder.

The man nodded in understanding and corralled the boys toward the stables. "Stop playing around and get your chores done. If I see one ceffyl in need of a meal, I'm feeding the laziest boy to her."

Hugging his wife to his chest, Mirek rushed to bring her inside. Under his breath, he whispered, "Your pains should be mine. I am the one who disobeyed the gods, not you. I don't understand why they have not accepted my atonement."

Her eyelids fluttered and she looked at him. He held his breath, hoping beyond anything that she'd say she forgave him. She made a weak noise and closed her eyes, whispering, "Aer in the mountains."

"Air in the mountains?" he questioned. "M'lady? I don't know what that means."

She had again lost consciousness.

Mirek brought her to the isolation chamber and laid her down. A servant had cleaned the blood from the floor and as a result the room smelled heavily of soap. Instantly, the medical unit turned on and began scanning her. He stepped back, watching the dance of green lasers against her forehead as the examination took place.

"Air in the mountains?" He shook his head. Was it a message from the gods? Was that how to keep her safe? And if the gods were giving him a clue, what in galaxy did it mean?

"Mountains," she mumbled the second the lasers finished their initial exam. Two metal plates slid up beside her head to fix the injury. He saw a blue light flash and had to close his eyes to the brightness of it.

"As you wish, my lady. We will find air in the mountains."

Her body seemed to visibly relax at the assurance.

Whatever that means, he thought, resuming his normal place seated on the floor against the hard wall.

RIONA JERKED VIOLENTLY as she came to full consciousness. Her head hit a medical panel. "Ow, blasted!" She lifted her hands to automatically cup her forehead and she banged her wrist onto the opposite side of the head panel.

"Easy, my lady."

Riona recognized the soothing voice. "What are you doing to me, dragon man?" The panel slid open, letting her see.

"I am Mirek. Your husband. Do you recognize me? You were struck on the head. How is your mind? Do you remember me?"

"Right, Mirek." Riona was captured by the clear color of green in his eyes. They were striking and the intensity in them left her a little breathless

—just like that first moment at the festival had. It was easy to see how he'd managed to seduce her into walking on stage with him. The details were still fuzzy, but she remembered going up there willingly to be presented before the crowd.

"You know me." He nodded, satisfied by this.

She pushed up so she wouldn't have to look directly at him. His nearness made her nervous. "Do your people greet everyone with rocks or am I just lucky?"

"They thought you were an alien."

"I am an alien," she answered wryly. "Do your people greet all *aliens* with rocks or am I just lucky?"

At that, he gave a small laugh. "I should have said an alien threat. We've had some issue with the Tyoe invading our mines. The boys are from Mining Village where the mines are located so they've heard the stories firsthand of what has happened."

Riona gasped in affront. "I look nothing like a Tyoe. They're giant balls of gelatinous goo."

"The boys have not seen them, only heard tales," Mirek defended. "And I don't know if you realize it, but you're not dressed according to your new home. In fact, those clothes are male and don't even belong to the same alien race."

"Hey, they fit me and I don't like dresses. The

skirts tangle in my legs and make running hard." Riona glanced over her attire. Seeing dirt on her arm, she absently brushed at it. The spot held her attention longer than it should have, but she found it easier than looking directly at dragon man's face.

"I will have breeches sewn for you."

"You don't have to do that." She glanced up through her lashes to look at him. "I don't have the space credit to pay for it right now."

"I will take care of it."

Did he have to be so accommodating? "That won't be necessary."

"I will not have my wife without clothes." A small smile formed on his mouth and his tone dropped. "At least, not outside of our home."

Riona shivered, not sure what to do with the sexual promise in his voice. She didn't have the necessary transmitters to exchange pleasure essences with him.

Oh, how she really wished she had the necessary transmitters to exchange pleasure essences with him. Riona tried to suppress the tingling of attraction in her stomach.

"I know you did not come to this planet with much. Galaxy Brides did not have belongings delivered for you as they did with some of the others. Whatever it is you have been through, you are safe here. I hope that you will tell me about it, about this Range you are afraid of, but I trust the gods knew what they were doing. We belong together, my lady. The details will work themselves out. I am just happy to see you awake after so many months."

"Months?" She looked at her arms. They still looked bad. "What do you mean months? What happened to me?"

Mirek gazed at her as if she was the prettiest woman in the universe. She felt a little self-conscious. Actually, how could he think that? She looked disease-ridden.

"Yes, months, but your readings look very good. I found you in the forest after the ceremony in a patch of the yellow. I had some of the best Medical Alliance doctors here to check on you. They believe it was a severe allergic reaction. In fact, they wish to do a medical study on you now that you are awake."

"No," she inserted quickly, holding up her hand. The last thing she needed was her name out on the waves. Range would be scanning for it and medical articles and newspaper chips were easy enough to pick up if you knew the frequencies to watch. "I don't want them to write about me. It's a, uh, religious thing. Besides, I don't want the entire universe knowing my personal business."

"As you wish, my lady, but I have called them back to examine you. I must insist they follow up your medical care. You were very ill. And as I said, Princess Nadja has sent natural medicines for you to try if you have pain. I'm told she comes from a family of doctors." Before she could deny him, he added, "So you enjoy running? Is that what you were doing in the forest?"

"Only when someone is chasing me," Riona mumbled before she could stop herself. She took a deep breath, trying to act confident. She'd seen her appearance. It was hard to act flippant and flirty when her skin was all marred up.

Mirek's mouth opened as if he'd question her.

"So, dragon man named Mirek," she put forth, walking out of the isolation chamber. The room was too small and this man too big in it.

"Yes, my lady?"

"Married, huh?" She made a great show of glancing around the room. As far as hideouts went, this one was pretty nice, and the bed beat snuggling into a hard shipping crate at night.

"Yes, my lady, we are married. The elders gave us their blessing. It is done." He followed her, trying to get close.

Riona kept moving, putting distance between them while trying to act nonchalant. "I don't remember there being much of a ceremony."

"It is true, we did not have the night in the tent together. I regret that our ceremony was not as it should be. You deserve better, my lady, but I will spend my life making it up to you."

"Yeah, I'm not really one for ceremonies," she dismissed.

"That is too bad. I thought perhaps once you were well, we could reenact the night in the tent." He looked hopeful.

Riona gave a small laugh. "I bet you would, dragon man." Then, lying, she said, "Unfortunately, nights in a tent are against my religion too."

"Then you were not raised like your sister after the Jagranst were destroyed? You were separated and put into a strict nunnery order?"

Riona froze. Her back was to him and she was glad for it. Tears instantly stung her eyes and she felt as if he'd kicked her. She couldn't breathe, couldn't move. The way he said her people's name, so lightly, as if watching an entire planet explode through a viewing portal on a space craft was just some story to be referenced. How could Aeron tell them? No one knew Riona was Jagranst. It was bad enough hearing the horror stories being told like some kind of myth to scare and entertain people. It was bad enough tolerating the jokes people made while having the memories locked away in her brain. "No. I am not like my sister."

She refused to say more about it. The pain choked her. She changed the course of the conversation. Hardening herself, she turned to face him. He sat on a bench seat near a small dining table.

"You know Aeron?" Riona inquired. This was the best piece of news she could have gotten. If he knew where Aeron was, it would save an aimless search over alien terrain.

"Of course, she married my brother Lord Bron, High Duke of the Draig."

"And you have spoken to her? Aeron has told you of the Tyoe attack?"

"Yes. The gods blessed us greatly. All three of my brothers found wives this year, as did my four prince cousins. Aeron told us of the attack and is helping us set up new communication networks. Clara, my brother Vlad's wife, has enlisted the help of her family to negotiate with the aliens and basically force them to leave us alone. She is Redde and their biological makeup hurts the Tyoe. The aliens ran for fear the Redde will destroy them. My brother Alek married Lady Kendall. She is helping us to clean up chemicals the Tyoe put in our mines before we knew of their presence."

Then there was no reason for her to remain here. She could get Aeron and go.

"The gods had their reasons for sending each bride to us," he continued. "I am not as familiar with the princesses, but I understand they are lovely ladies. Princess Nadja has worked on your medical problem. Princess Pia—"

"Pia?" Riona repeated, remembering the beast of the man who'd hauled her across the festival grounds on his shoulder. "That man she was with is a prince?"

"Prince Zoran. He is Captain of the Guards near the palace. A very fine warrior." Mirek continued conversationally. "You might remember Princess Morrigan, they call her Rigan, from the ship as well. And Princess Olena has often asked about you."

"I like Olena. We spent a lot of time together on the ship," Riona said absently. Then, holding his gaze with her intense one, she asked seriously. "Is my sister is safe?"

"Yes, my lady, very. She visits you every day. She came to see you when I told her you'd awoken, but you were passed out on the floor. She will be back later when you are up for visitors."

Aeron was safe. The tension rolled out of her body by small degrees. She took a deep breath, feeling that the pain in her chest had lessened. "I want to see her."

"I'll let her know." The conversation lagged into a slightly awkward silence.

"It sounds like all the brides have been beneficial to your people," Riona said to fill the quiet, "but the gods had no use for me and made me sleep." She meant it to be a joke, but she couldn't quite manage the playful, carefree smile. Riona was instantly sorry.

His expression fell. "That is my fault. I should not have pushed for a wedding so quickly. I should have waited a year. But it is done now, and I hope you can forgive me."

Mirek stared at her expectantly. Riona slowly nodded, unsure how to respond. She was still trying to get used to the fact she had somehow gotten married—not that she considered this a real marriage. She couldn't help his customs and what he believed, but she hadn't agreed to be a wife.

Marriage meant family and roots and love. Those were all things she did not want. If she thought she was in love, she'd run. She'd get on the fastest ship she could find and she'd disappear. Love meant pain. Families died. Roots withered. Nothing stayed as it should be. The only option was to live fluid, cascading over the rocks in her path, never stopping. She was a stream, crashing through the universe. Mirek was a rock, rooted here on one planet. It didn't matter that he had kind eyes and a handsome face. Soon, like everyone else, he'd be a memory. All she had was Aeron—the last remnant of a sad past—and Riona needed it to remain that way.

"Do you forgive me?" he asked again, as if determining the weak gesture wasn't enough.

Riona nodded again. "Of course. You were only doing what you thought you had to."

And I will do what I must to protect my sister and myself, she thought.

6

"Ri? Wake up."

Riona blinked open her eyes at the beckoning of the familiar voice. "Aer?"

"Yes, it's Aeron."

A hand touched Riona's face. Her sister's face came into view as Aeron leaned over her.

"I found you." Riona pushed up from the bed and wrapped her arms around her sister. Mirek had left her alone to sleep and, though the light in the bedroom was dim, she could make out her sister's face. "Are you hurt? I saw that man carrying you off." She pulled back to study Aeron. "Did he…?" Riona looked down, instantly seeing her sister's large belly. Aeron was pregnant. "No. What did he do to you?"

"He is a wonderful man." Aeron grabbed her hands and squeezed them. "I'm so happy."

"I'll kill him!" A tear slipped over Riona's cheek and landed on the green material of Aeron's dress, darkening it. "You're dying. He's killed you."

"It's life," Aeron corrected. "You should feel when the baby moves. I don't feel like I'm dying. I feel alive."

Riona withdrew from her sister. The look of pure happiness on Aeron's face was all wrong. Her sister wasn't happy, not like this. Then, looking at the stomach, she frowned. "How far along are you?"

"It's almost time. I was so worried you wouldn't be awake for it." Aeron rubbed her stomach.

"All right, we can figure this out." Riona stood and began to pace. "I'll take care of you. We'll find a way off this planet and I'll help you. I'll raise the baby. And when you…when you…oh, blessed stars, when you're no longer with us, I will be there for the child."

"I'm not on death's door."

"You know what having sex does to our kind. We're Jagranst, Aeron. We're the last of our people." Riona stared at her sister, feeling time slip away. "At best you can hope to have, what? Forty, fifty more years?"

"I don't think it's true. I think we were always going to die. The elders probably told us that to keep us out of the beds of boys since we were so young. The boys didn't want to be accused of murder, so they didn't try to seduce us. My husband has contacted a lot of doctors about it. They've looked at our genetics. The Jagranst are an offset of human. As far as I am able to piece together, our ancestors went to the planet to escape the corruption of Old Earth human society. There was nothing spectacular—genetically speaking—about our people. It was but a story to keep kids in line."

"You called him your husband?" Riona tried to take in everything that was happening. Nothing made sense. "You've accepted it?"

"I love him, Ri." Aeron smiled, looking so hopeful. "These are really good people. I know you're going to like them as I do. Mirek has been so worried about you. I never thought you'd get married too, but you have chosen very well. Your husband is a good man."

Riona didn't know how to respond. She stood in the middle of the room, feeling like her life had become a strange play. If she didn't move it would be over and she could resume normality.

"I know we haven't always been close in the past, but that's about to change." Aeron got up from the bed and came to her. "We have a second chance here."

Riona looked at the pregnant belly. Aeron was right. They hadn't been close as adults. However, that did not change the fact that Riona knew her sister. This was not Aeron. This excited, bubbly, pregnant, unconcerned creature was not her sister. Riona was positive she could sleep for fifty years and Aeron would not be this changed.

"What about the aliens?" Riona asked. "The Tyoe might come back."

"The threat has been averted. We did it. The planet is safe. All know of your part in it. You got me here to protect them. Already they look at you as family. The locals are kind and so giving. I can't wait for you to meet them."

Riona rubbed her head. The bump from the rock was gone. "Oh, I met the welcoming party."

Aeron ignored her ill humor. "Our sister Clara has visited you every day. Kendall checks on you often."

"Kendall doesn't like me. I know that much from the ship," Riona disputed.

Aeron was supposed to be somber and moody and judgmental. She didn't embrace motherhood and wifehood. She liked her little room on her little Federation ship, living in her little lonely air pocket of a life.

"Why are you looking at me like that?" Aeron tilted her head in question and placed a hand protectively over her stomach.

"I don't feel like myself," Riona lied.

Aeron's smile fell some but she nodded. "I understand. You look better. We are all very happy you're awake. Mirek has been taking very good care of you, even going to the temple to pray to his gods every chance he gets. Who knows, maybe it worked. You're awake."

"How did I fall asleep?"

"The best anyone could tell is that you had a severe allergic reaction to something they call the yellow. It's a plant found in the forest by the palace. The pollen can render someone unconscious if they breathe it in."

"Allergies?" Riona looked at her arm. Splotches still marred her flesh but they had faded to a light pink. The explanation sounded questionable to her.

"I couldn't believe it either. With everything we know about illnesses and plagues, the Medical Alliance couldn't pull you out of an allergy coma." Aeron lifted her hand to touch Riona's cheek.

Riona automatically stiffened at the gesture. "What have you done with my sister?"

"What? Ri, what are you saying?" Aeron frowned.

Riona pointed at Aeron before ticking points

off on her fingers. "My sister never acts like you do. My sister doesn't marry people. My sister doesn't live on an alien world. My sister is not pregnant. My sister can't stand to be in the same room with me for longer than a minute. She always lectures me. She's so by-the-book Federation it's disgusting. So either you're an imposter, or you're under the influence of that crazy Killing Maiden wine we drank at the festival."

"Maiden's Last Breath," Aeron calmly corrected. "And I don't drink liquor. I'm pregnant."

"Correcting me is the first Aeron thing you've done. My sister always has to be right." Riona placed her hands on her hips and glared at the woman. She wanted to feel normal. Arguing with Aeron was just that—normal. "Two days ago, you were lecturing me about being irresponsible. You threatened to have me arrested for forging your name on a bridal procurement contract."

"That was months—"

"It was two days for me, Federation." Riona expected a fight from her baiting. She was disappointed.

Aeron slowly nodded and took a step back. "I'm sorry. I didn't realize you thought I was so horrible." Turning, she made her way to the stairs.

Riona watched her sister walk away. Actually, it

was more a strange shuffling motion. Sighing, she made a move to follow. "Aeron, wait."

Aeron lifted her hand and shook her head, not bothering to turn around.

Riona let her go. To herself, she mumbled sarcastically, "Well played, Ri. You attacked a pregnant woman."

The long shirt she wore to bed went to her thighs. Not really thinking about what she was doing, she went to the wardrobe to change her clothes. To her surprise, she found pants in her size had been placed next to the gowns. They hung loose around the legs and pulled together with a drawstring. Matching tunic shirts hung on hooks. They were simple in design but very well made.

When she walked down the stairs, she hoped to see her sister waiting for her. Instead, Mirek glanced up from a hand-held unit. He sat on the couch, one ankle crossed over a knee. His pants looked like hers, but he wore a Fajerkin tight shirt and long-brimmed hat with sweeping feather that framed his face. Riona arched a brow but said nothing as she made her way to a tray of food left on a table. Whatever she had been tube eating the last several months was wearing off and she felt the first pangs of hunger in her stomach.

"Lord Mirek?" the hand-held inquired.

Mirek turned his attention back. "My apologies, Jerk. I am communicating from home today. My wife was ill but is better now."

Riona stiffened and snapped her head to look at him.

"My lady, please," Mirek looked at her and gestured that she should come toward him.

Riona looked behind her, though she knew very well there was no one else in the home with them. She ran her fingers through what had to be a mess of hair and hesitated before moving forward. Mirek turned the hand-held viewing screen toward her. A Fajerkin nobleman waited expectantly. Riona stiffened, waiting for the man to recognize her. His hat was like Mirek's only with two feathers signifying his great rank amongst his people.

Mirek started to speak, but Riona interrupted him. "A pleasure, Jerk." She rolled her hand in the air and touched her chin to her chest. The noble returned the greeting.

Mirek smiled and moved the hand-held camera around to again pick up his conversation. Riona listened for her name, but they didn't mention her. Instead, they negotiated ore trade. The Fajerkin people owned a few fueling docks. When Mirek ended the transmission, he pulled the hat from his head.

"You just made a deal for a hundred-thousand space credits with one communication," Riona said, unable to hide her surprise. "From your couch."

She didn't care much for the hat, but the tight shirt did have some appeal. Her breathing deepened and she forced herself to look away from the dragon man's chest to the food. Suddenly, she wasn't as hungry. Her heart quickened and a small tremor worked its way up her legs. She wasn't an idiot. She knew what attraction was. Of course, she'd never felt it so deeply before, but that could be because anytime she was attracted to a man she ran the other way—not giving herself time to feel it.

"I did. They're a smaller account, but they like to negotiate large orders at one time and spread the delivery out over the year." He lifted the hat, shook it lightly so the feather danced and then tossed it next to him on the seat while adding, "It almost makes wearing this thing worth it."

"They why do you? I know for a fact the Fajerkin noblemen wouldn't put on Draig clothing. You should wear yours, as he wears his."

"I find it puts others at ease during negations. Plus, I make them fly here to pick up their ore since we don't deliver out of our airspace. So it is a gesture of goodwill and respect."

"Well, you won't find me wearing Fajerkin attire anytime soon." Riona sat on the bench seat next to the table. A hundred thousand in one deal? So much money. Mirek acted like the sum was an afterthought, barely worth working for. She thought of Range. Riona desperately needed to find a way to pay him off. Surely these people wouldn't miss fifty-thousand, not when they made deals like this every day.

Too bad I'm not that kind of thief, she thought. Naturally, she wanted to take the money and run, but she wouldn't. She had standards.

Mirek tilted his head thoughtfully. "I don't believe I've ever met a Fajerkin woman before."

"You wouldn't have." Riona looked at the food but didn't touch it. "They keep them locked up with chains and little to no clothing."

"I try not to judge how others do things, but that is startling news." Mirek made his way toward the table and sat across from her. She wished he hadn't. When he was close she found it hard to concentrate. He continued, "The food is for you. Lady Aeron brought it. She thought they were flavors you might like. You sister has become quite the cook."

An assortment of cooked meat slices, cut blue bread, crusted pastries and tiny round fruits were arranged prettily on a tray. Riona merely stared at it.

"You should probably refrain from introducing me to your trade contacts in the future," she said.

"You say you forgive me, but you have not." He slowly nodded as if he understood. "What is it you would have me do? Find a cave in the mountains? We can leave today if that is what you wish. Will the mines do, or would you rather it be a natural cave?"

Riona frowned and rubbed behind her ear. Cave in the mountains? Was her universal translator broken? She'd won it in a game of chance, but still, it had never failed her. Then, realizing he spoke the old star language, which didn't need translating, she answered, "I told you I forgive you. I see no reason to go underground unless I'm on the run from the authorities."

His pleasant expression wavered. That comment affected him, though he tried hard to hide his worry. "Do you often find yourself on the run from the authorities?"

"Define often." She reached for the tray and forced herself to take a small piece of fruit. The sweet flavor exploded in her mouth.

"More than three times in the last ten years," he supplied.

"Then yes," Riona gave a small laugh. "Very often. Though to be fair, authorities is a very subjective term. Some people call themselves an authority, but I don't necessarily recognize their authority over me."

"But you do intend to obey the laws of your new world, do you not?" Mirek's eyes stayed steadily on her, piercing in their green intensity. She tried to avoid eye contact by looking at the food tray. "We are nobles. Others will look to us to see how to act. Honor and duty are a part of the title. I am Ealdorman of Draig and, as my wife, you are Lady Riona."

In her nervousness, she ate a little too quickly and began to cough. She? A noblewoman? The idea was hysterical in and of itself. She cleared her throat. "I can't really say. I don't know all of your planet's laws."

"Our planet. Qurilixen in your home now."

Riona's hand stopped mid action and she dropped the piece of fruit pinched between her fingers. Even now, in this moment, the sight of the explosion was clear in her mind. She didn't want a home world, not ever again. "It's a kind offer."

"You do not sound pleased." Mirek reached his hand to stop the discarded fruit from rolling off the table.

"I'm trying to be polite."

"I would rather you speak honestly than politely. How else are we to learn about each other and fall into a happy marriage?" There was that hopeful look again. Did the man have to be so positive?

He wanted honesty? Okay. Wish granted. "That Fajerkin noble you were speaking to, I don't remember his name."

"Jerk Kando," Mirek said. "I was very impressed with your knowledge of their greeting. You questioned why the gods sent you here. Perhaps your skills will compliment mine as Mining Ambassador."

"You run the ore mines?" Riona swallowed nervously. Just how powerful was this husband of hers?

"Control of the mines is a long-held tradition with my family. It ensures the king and his sons have full focus on the enemy Var who live to the south of the palace. My brother Vlad handles the day-to-day operations onworld. He is Ealdorman Honorary of Draig and the High Mining Official. As the offworld ambassador, it is my duty to see to trade negotiations, orders, shipping, payments, and politics. We have a launch pad and fleet of ships here in the mountain fortress. A few alien ambassadors land, such as the Redde, who are here visiting their daughter, Lady Clara. For the most part, we greet them in space and keep work off the planet. The locals prefer it that way. Not many know of the Fajerk greeting. If you are skilled in alien customs, it will be a great asset to our people."

"Yeah," Riona drawled. "I wouldn't be so quick to assume as much. You're lucky the Jerk didn't recognize me."

"Why?"

"A ship I happened to be on crashed into a fuel station's communications tower. The station was owned by Kando's brother. They tried to force us to pay for the damage, but it was determined they had drifted a parsec out of their assigned territory and thus couldn't insist we compensate them for damages since they were not where they should have been. We left before the Federation could get involved." She studied him. He didn't move, merely fingered the piece of fruit in his hand, as if testing its firmness. The slow motion of his fingers made the trembling inside her start anew. "Fajerk is a small planet and I believe I'm still on their wanted list. So you see, as long as I don't land there, I'm technically not under their authority. However, if they see you married me, it's possible they'll try to maneuver to get me in their custody."

"If you damaged property, you should compensate them for it."

"I didn't say it was my proudest moment," she mumbled. "They have insurance. They wanted a double payday. And they shouldn't have been there."

"And how did you crash? Was your ship damaged?"

"I bet the pilot he couldn't fly blindfolded. Turned out I was right." She gave a light shrug. "If they had been where they were supposed to be, it would have been fine."

"A bet?"

"I said I wasn't proud of it," she answered through clenched teeth. "I don't live my life apologizing for who or what I am, or for what I've done. Frankly, there is only one person in all the universes who I care about—my sister."

"That is a cold view, my lady. It saddens me that you would have it."

It was better he knew the truth. He seemed to really believe in this destiny nonsense. If there were gods moving the population around like little pieces in a game, gambling with people's lives, she wanted no part of their ill-fated playtime. They had destroyed everything.

"It is what it is," Riona said. "That's it. Aeron is all I have room for inside my heart."

"Then why did you send her away crying?"

"Crying?" Riona glanced at the door leading from his home as if she'd be able to determine for herself if he spoke the truth. "Aeron never cries."

"She was after she left you."

Guilt racked her. She pressed a nail into the webbing between her thumb and forefinger until it hurt. "What did your people do to her?"

"We gave her a home, a family, a life. All that we have is hers, as it is yours if you allow it to be."

"No." She shook her head in denial. "I know my sister." She pointed at the door. "That's not my sister."

"Perhaps she suffers from the joys of pregnancy."

"Joys?" Riona shot to her feet. "You mean *horror*. Pregnancy is a death sentence for our kind. Well, not necessarily the pregnancy itself but the sex to get pregnant."

When Aeron died, she'd be the only one left. Forever. Tears burned her nose and her eyes but she refused to cry. It was unknown if the baby would take after them. By all accounts, the Draig only produced male children. A boy wouldn't have the same lifespan as a female Jagranst.

"Joys is a polite way of saying pregnancy hormones." Mirek remained calm.

Riona found his persistent niceness irritated her. She wanted him to tirade and act like an ass… mainly so it would excuse her behavior.

"Because of Aeron's concern, and because you are sisters and my wife, and because you were sick,

I had the Medical Alliance doctors run the same tests on you as they did Aeron. You are genetically human. They could find no medical reason as to why you would be immortal, let alone how that immortality would be tied to your sexual practices." He stood and went back to the couch. Lifting the hand-held he'd been using to communicate with earlier, he pressed the screen and then handed it to her. Riona instantly recognized it to be a medical report. "Everything is right there."

Hadn't Aeron said the same thing? She didn't want to believe it, but what if it was true? If she was genetically human then that meant… "I'm dying too."

"Not for a long time," he said, clearly trying to be comforting. "You are a very tough woman. Just look how sick you were a few days ago and now you are almost completely healed."

Riona scrolled over the report, picking up keywords and stopping once she'd arrived at the summary. Her eyes turned from the words on the screen to her arm. Her skin did look better. She touched it with shaking fingers as if feeling it for the first time. "Mortal."

"Yes." Mirek nodded. "But you have many years left, more so now that you are my wife. My life force is yours. Your new home world is special. The blue sun's radiation—"

"Mortal," she repeated, not really hearing him. "I'm mortal."

MIREK FORCED himself to meet his wives tortured eyes. Why had he given her the medical reports? Yes, she had a right to know, but the look on her face tore at his heart. Everything in him wanted to hold her, but he forced himself to be patient.

For months, he sat by her side, worrying for her. He had become used to the idea of her, of them. And, oh, how he was ready for their lives together to start. Months of unspoken conversations welled inside him. He'd thought of many things he wanted to tell her. Stories he wanted her to know—anecdotes from his youth, tales of his meetings with bizarre aliens, dreams of their future together. In his mind she knew everything about him. He'd imagined her answers.

Maybe he'd gone mad, creating a life with an unconscious woman. His expectations of her, combined with his imagination of what she would be, caused his conversation to be stunted. He could greet any alien dignitary with ease. He could read faces and gestures even when the person was from a culture very unlike his. It was a strange sixth sense he'd been born with. It made him a great ambassador for his people. Yet here, presented with his wife who was by all rights chosen for him by the gods, he couldn't manage to make his words flow.

"It's true," Riona stated, looking again at his hand-held. "I was always going to die."

"I shouldn't have told you." It was more of a question than a statement.

"Are you kidding? This is great news."

That was not the reaction he'd expected from someone who'd just found out they were suddenly mortal.

"I feel like this weight of expectation has been lifted off me." Riona breathed heavily. She shook her hands in front of her with nervous energy as she stood and began to pace. "I'm going to die someday and there is nothing I can do about it. Here I've been forcing myself to live for a dead planet when it turns out my existence is out of my hands." Her beautiful face turned toward him once more. "I have lived my entire life taking risks, seeking excitement, living for those who no longer could, in what I really think might have been an attempt to take the pressure off. I don't want to be dead, but if I died by accident having fun, then…" She took several more deep breaths. He wondered if she was about to hyperventilate. Before he could ask, she rushed on, "but in the process I've been avoiding what I've been told is one of the best things in the known universe."

"Chocolate?" he asked, attempting a joke to lighten the mood. "I'm told by women it's as close to bliss as they can get."

"Oh, I've had chocolate. I won an entire vat of chocolate off some monks." To his surprise, she began pulling off her shirt.

"Do you need—" he gestured weakly toward the isolation room, "—mental, ah, medical help?"

"I have wanted to press against you since I first saw you. Do you know what it's like living with the responsibility of a dead civilization on your head? Thinking to touch and kiss and feel another person would be betraying their legacy?" Suddenly, she paused with her shirt clutched in her fist. "You do want me, right? I mean, you want to be married to me so I assumed that translated into you wanting to be in my bed."

Unable to help himself, he stared at her naked chest. If he looked close enough he could see patches of light pink where the blisters had been. It didn't matter. She was the most beautiful thing he'd ever seen and she was offering herself to him. His body lurched with excitement and for a moment he couldn't move, couldn't speak. This was not how he'd expected things to go. Mirek realized his mouth was open and licked his dry lips before closing it. He nodded, unable to form a vocal answer.

"Oh, good." She sighed in relief. Riona pushed her pants off her hips. Then, standing before him completely naked, she commanded, "All right. Do it."

"Do...?" He stood.

"Yes. Do the thing."

"Thing?"

"Yes, do the thing, sex, get naked," she gestured that he should start.

Mirek reached for the tight shirt and pulled it over his head. He placed it on the table. Every part of him wanted to surge forward, but he had paid dearly for his impatience the day they married. He would not act in haste again. "I think you may be reacting badly to the medical news."

"I admit, my experience in these types of matters is fairly nonexistent. But it seems to me that you have a woman standing naked in front of you, ready to be sexed on and you are still dressed." She arched a challenging brow. "I mean, if you're not up for it, I'm sure someone will be willing to misbehave with me. I have all this energy that needs to find an outlet. I need to do something before it makes me crazy. So either we have sex, or I'm going to steal a spaceship and go for a joyride. You decide."

Mirek felt a strange blend of excitement and concern filling him. This woman was nothing like he'd imagined. He saw the mischief in her eyes. She liked games. She liked adrenaline. She liked playing with fire.

"Come on, dragon man—" she pouted, "—make with the naughtiness."

Mirek could only take so much teasing. He'd wanted her since he first saw her, and the months of waiting had been hell. Then there were the years of failed festivals before that. He rushed forward. She made a small noise of surprise as he grabbed her arms. His lips met hers in an instantly deep kiss. The taste of her fruit-sweetened lips drew his tongue forward.

For an instant, she didn't respond, merely stood frozen in place as he released his passion onto her. The dragon in him loved the challenge. The man in him warned him to slow down. She may be willing, but her culture had insured she had little experience. Mirek couldn't really care less if he had a virgin bride. It was something he'd never really thought about in his years of waiting to be blessed, for he knew when the time came his wife would be all his and sexual pasts didn't matter.

She pulled her head back and gasped for breath. "Go easy, dragon." Gentle hands cupped his face and the caress instantly encouraged him to slow. There was a vulnerability in her he'd never detected before. His wife had many layers, and he was eager to discover them all.

Mirek relaxed his grip on her arms and moved his fingers up along her throat. Before he felt the hard thread of her pulse, he heard it in his head. His senses were keenly aware, though he did not shift into dragon. The Draig did not make love in dragon form but they could use its power of enhanced senses. Mirek smelled her desire for him. He tasted her sweet lips like fine fruit wine. Her body trembled beneath his touch, the softness of her naked flesh against his chest and stomach. The deep intake of her breath whispered past his lips, almost tickling him.

Never in his life had he felt so connected to another person. It was a primal thing, innate, beyond conscious understanding. Tiny, invisible threads joined them, pulling them together from that very first moment he looked at her. His crystal had glowed and he'd just known she was meant for him. It was this pull that had made him claim her, and now that he kissed her the feelings only intensified. She was his destiny. The gods knew what they were doing.

Riona had absolutely no idea what she was doing. As she'd stared at the medical report, years of pent-up frustration and stress had released inside her. She'd been living with a giant anvil over her head, secretly wishing that fate would take her long life out of her hands. The knowledge of her freedom from her past flowed through her. Even if the reports were wrong, maybe it was time to start her biological countdown and live out a natural humanoid existence.

When Mirek's lips touched hers, it felt right. Actually, it felt wicked and wonderful. The shock of his warm skin to her breasts caused tiny explosions of pleasure to erupt beneath her flesh. She'd had pleasure before, but never from actual physical contact with a man.

Mirek slid his hands to her breasts, cupping them before gliding lower to her hips. He pulled her firmly against him. The hard length of his arousal beneath his breeches pressed along her stomach. Riona wasn't one to back down from adventure. By the way her heart thudded in her chest and her blood raced in her veins this was definitely an adventure.

He stepped forward, forcing her to walk back toward the couch. When her naked ass hit the furniture, she tried to pull away. Before she could lie down, he swept her into his arms and changed directions. She bounced in his arms. A small laugh escaped her as he took the stairs leading to the bedroom.

The shades were still drawn from when she'd been sleeping and the dim light added an intimate atmosphere to the moment. He placed her on the bed. Each of his movements seemed strained, as if he held back. Despite all her brave teasing, she was glad he was gentle with her. This was new territory.

He crawled over her and kissed her lips as if that single act was the most important thing in the world. Mirek wrapped his arms behind her back, holding her tight as he lifted her shoulders off the mattress. "Are you sure this is what you want? This is not a reaction to shock from reading the reports?"

Her arms were trapped between them, but she managed to caress his jaw with her fingertips. "This is the one adventure in my life I thought I could never have. We're adults. I'm willing. You're willing."

"We're married," he inserted.

"Ah, well..." She looked to the side and scrunched up her nose. "I won't lie to you. I really have no intention of being married."

"But...?" In his surprise, his hold loosened and she fell back on the bed. Her head bounced on the mattress but it didn't hurt. "The gods have shown us. My crystal glowed when I saw you. Didn't you feel the pull?"

Riona had felt it, so much so that she'd mindlessly followed him on stage. "I already admitted I was attracted to you. I think it was your eyes. They're so gorgeous. And you are very physically pleasing to look at. If you want the truth, I think you are confusing lust with love, or at least with the will of the gods. I'm not judging you for it. You can't really help that there are not a lot of females on this planet for you to have fun with. As for me, I have only had intimacy with transmitters meant for long-distance lovers."

"But tradition, the gods…"

"Maybe your people made up traditions to ensure you married with little fuss, just as mine made up traditions to keep young adults from fooling around." Riona saw her logic hurt him. This was not the conversation she wanted to be having. But he'd given her a dose of reality. Perhaps he needed one as well.

He closed his eyes and held his breath. She wondered at it but said nothing. Her body tingled where he touched her. The heat of his leg combined with the tickle of his breeches to tease her sex. When he opened his eyes, he said, "My impatience did this. I should have been stronger and waited for the next festival to claim you. This is why you doubt me and cannot feel our connection."

The feelings of arousal built. She couldn't seem to control her leg as she restlessly caressed his hip with her thigh. The muscles of his chest beckoned her hands to explore. There were so many emotions inside of her that she couldn't filter them all. Relief was the most prevalent—relief that she was not immortal. Then there was lust, a hard desire as if her brain's tight hold on her body had finally given way, bestowing its silent permission to allow her to feel. Beneath that was uncertainty and worry mixed with a tiny thread of fear that this was all a joke and the Draig had her sister under a spell and was trying to do the same to her. If a yellow plant could make her that sick, what else did these guys have on their planet that could affect her?

His body responded to her thigh's persistence and he rocked his hips forward. Lust overtook all else and suspicions simply fell out of her head.

"Logic tells me to wait, but when I am with you, patience never seems to be an option." He circled his hips again. "These months have been torture—seeing you hurt and unable to do anything about it." He pressed harder, simulating the sexual act through his clothes. "And now having you here, naked, willing to take me in you." He thrust again, gasping and shivering. "If this is a test from the gods, I fear I will fail."

"Can we leave them out of it?" she asked, her muscles tightening. "I really don't want to think about supreme beings right now."

He reached for his waist, and seconds later her thighs were able to work the material off his hips. The brush of hard naked flesh created a myriad of unexpected sensations. His arousal fit against her sex, sliding in her body's natural response. With an artful motion, he readjusted his hips to bring the head of his shaft to her opening. She stiffened in anticipation. Her heart beat so loud she couldn't hear anything else.

Mirek slipped inside her, letting her feel the tip of him. The cords in his neck were strained, attesting to the fact he held back. Riona closed her eyes and drew her hips up to search for more. The small physical discomfort was nothing compared to the pleasure. He withdrew only to come back a little deeper. It took a few strokes, but she learned his rhythm and met it with her own.

Mirek held his weight off her by pressing his hands into the mattress by her side. She wanted more and tried to force him deeper with the thrust of her body. When he would pull away, she wrapped her legs around him and held tight. The motion had the added benefit of angling her body to compel him deeper.

His eyes rounded. She locked her ankles and kept him from withdrawing. As her sex adjusted, she couldn't help but rock her hips in tiny circles. He stayed deep, his body filling and caressing her in a way she'd never dreamed possible. The faster she rocked, the better it felt, and the more torturous.

Mirek took her lead, pushing back to grab her hips. The motion lifted her off the bed and onto his lap. He sat back on his feet as her legs were forced to release his waist. Gravity locked her onto his shaft, helped by the forceful grasp of his hands. He kept her tight against him, letting her have only the smallest of movements inside her sex.

Riona leaned her face into his. The sides of their noses touched. She panted for air as his breath fanned over her cheek. Deep green eyes looked into hers. Though the room was shadowed, she detected the brightness of them. She loved their color, the starkness of it, the piercing intensity that shot through her and enhanced the pleasure in her stomach.

Her heart beat fiercely and she felt the familiar rush of excitement that overtook her whenever she was about to do something marvelously wild—win a tournament, sneak though security, fly a landship at lightning speeds. The rush in her veins made her feel alive.

The pleasure built. Her body jerked almost violently. She gave a weak cry and deep tremors exploded between them. Mirek's breath caught and his head fell back. He became stiff and then gripped her hard.

Their mingled breaths filled the silence. He let go and she slipped off his lap and fell weakly into bed. Mirek collapsed next to her, lying on his back.

"That was better than a trip through the Jeyer Obstacle," she panted, unable to help the wide smile.

"I have no idea what that is, but I'll take it as a compliment." He turned his head so he faced her.

Riona met his gaze. Deep relaxation turned her bones to liquid and her limbs to useless weights. "Yes. It's a good thing, dragon man, a very good thing. And it's something I think we should do again very soon."

A low growl sounded in the back of his throat. She inhaled sharply in surprise as he pushed up and over her with lightning speed only to begin eagerly kissing her neck. "As my lady wishes."

7

"WHAT HAPPENED TO YOU?" Alek eyed Mirek in concern. "Did you have to wrestle negotiate with the Syog again?"

"My wife." Mirek stopped his slow, ambling walk and leaned against the corridor wall. Not that he would complain, but Riona had taken to intimacy with a vivacious force he'd ever dreamed possible. "She's, ah, fully recovered now."

Alek quirked a brow. It took him a long moment to understand what was happening. His concern turned into hard, full laughter. He clutched his stomach and bent over, struggling to breathe.

"What's going on out here?" Bron appeared from the scroll room, holding a stack of yellowed parchments. He eyed his brothers curiously.

"Lady…learned…sex…balls," was about all of Alek's answer they could understand.

Mirek grimaced. He should have known better than to admit soreness to one of his brothers. Why hadn't he lied and said he'd been getting his privates kicked in a Syog ball racking negotiation? It would have been an easy lie. Those aliens were rough on the manhood, even if they used a semi-protective plate. No one would have questioned his claim. They would have still laughed at him, but they would have believed him.

"Mirek?" Bron asked in concern.

"Riona, ah—" Mirek began.

"He can't handle…his wife," Alek interrupted in merriment. "He's walking like this." Alek ambled around the hall like an old man with a cane, stumbling all the more in his fit of laughter.

Bron arched a brow and nodded his head. "Nicely done. We'll have another nephew to add to the family soon. Well done, brother."

"If she didn't break him," Alek inserted. "I always suspected you were a little soft, Ambassador. All that flying in space and drinking lady wine with the aliens."

Mirek shoved Alek into a wall. It didn't stop the laughter as the man slid to the floor. "At least I don't smell like a ceffyl herd."

"I deserve that," Alek admitted, not bothering to stand as he grinned up at them. A change had come over him since his marriage. He was happier and smiled more. Whatever Kendall had done to her husband, she'd managed to tame the stubborn man.

"You're going to tell everyone, aren't you?" Mirek sighed, not really worried. His wife wanted him. That was a good thing. Actually, she wanted him…and wanted him…and wanted him…and—

"Oh, yeah," Alek nodded. "Everyone."

"Alek," Bron broke in. "Maybe we should keep this to ourselves. If my wife is any indication of how the women were raised, her sister will not like being talked about in such a way. She will consider it insulting."

Alek instantly agreed. "Of course, I didn't think of it like that. I would never gossip about my sisters if it made them uncomfortable."

"Thank you," Mirek mouthed. Bron nodded once.

"Have either of you seen the updated communications plans?" Bron asked, nodding at his armload. "We're having a hard time locating some of the buried mountain lines to see if they're salvageable. Aeron wants to get the construction plans finished before the baby arrives and keeps asking if they're lines or transmit boosters. I honestly have no idea how they work."

"Why don't you just grab a line on one side and pull?" Alek asked, shrugging. "See where it leads. If it doesn't lead anywhere, I'd say we have transmit boosters. I don't know what a transmit booster looks like, but we can send the boys out to look for one in the trees or wherever."

"Apparently checking the line that way will take longer. Aeron ordered a ground imager but it won't be here until after the baby comes. She is *very* focused on getting this done. Now." Bron looked at them hopefully, an almost desperate plea on his face as he wanted to please his pregnant wife. "So have you seen the updated plans?"

"Updated as in the ones from fifty years ago?" Mirek frowned. "Did we even have plans? I don't ever remember seeing them. I seem to remember Sper just making it work. He'd go out with tools and come back later with everything working again."

"Alek?" Bron prompted.

"No clue," Alek said. "I think Sper kept all the plans in his head. When he died, he took the information with him. Though, come to think of it, after he died the network stopped breaking down so much. I wonder what that man was doing?"

"Intergalactic transmissions," Mirek answered. Sper never married, never even tried to marry. He was a very rare exception to the Draig culture in that way. "Something he called moving, moodies, movies?"

"Blast!" Bron frowned. "That's what I was afraid of. Aeron is not going to be pleased. She is a very organized woman." To Mirek, he said, "She was always like that, but it's getting worse. At first, she just arranged clothing in the closet according to styles and color. But then I caught her trying to alphabetize your giant trade agreement reports in my office in the middle of the night."

"Wait until your bride starts hiding your favorite throwing knives," Alek said. "I wish Kendall would merely reorganize reports."

"I believe that is part of the joys of pregnancy," Mirek offered. "I'm told women do that kind of thing."

"Kendall is doing many strange things. When I threw a couple knives in the house she scolded me for ruining the wood on the new throwing post. Then she tried to take away all the sharp objects and put them really high in the home so not even I could reach them. How's it going to be a throwing post if I can't put weapons in it and soften it up for my boy to learn? And how is my son going to reach the weapons if they're glued to the ceiling? You'd almost think she didn't want the child to have a sharp blade." Alek took a deep breath and lowered his voice to a near whisper. "Then, as I'm rubbing her wonderful giant belly and tell her I want at least thirteen children, she tried to hit me with a plate of chocolate and an ore sample she was looking at. My Kendall is not a violent lady."

The fathers-to-be shook their heads, completely at a loss.

"One visiting dignitary told me he and his wife called it nesting," Mirek said. "Toward the end time women start doing strange things to the home. They can't help it. You should probably help them. I don't like the idea of my pregnant sisters climbing high and lifting heavy objects. They seem a little off balance of late when they simply walk down the hall."

"Like a baldric slaughtering prey to make nest bedding," Alek concluded. "That actually makes complete sense. Perhaps that is why she is putting the knives up high. She's building a nest."

"Nesting. Aeron has been taking all the covers and pillows and surrounding herself with them at night. And quite frankly, some of the strange things she's been eating resemble food a baldric might enjoy—not in taste so much, but it looks disgusting.

I think you may be right, Mirek. We should find a way to help them with this nesting process." Bron shared a determined look with Alek.

"At times like this I miss our mother. She would have told us what to do," Mirek said.

"How hard can it be to build a nest?" Bron's bearing seemed lighter than before. "Mirek, thank you. I'm glad someone in this family understands these women things."

Alek stood and spoke toward Bron. "You know, now that Mirek has something else to occupy his time, I'm guessing we can finally tell him we don't really read those report things. No reports, nothing for your wife to organize."

Mirek's expression fell. "What? You nagged me for months to make fully detailed accountings of my trade missions and then you begged me for more…"

Bron smirked and looked guiltily away. Alek began laughing anew.

"Do you know how tediously boring those things are to write?" Mirek demanded.

"Not as boring as it is to read all two hundred pages of them," Alek answered.

"You had me inserting dignitary eye color and breathing patterns," Mirek growled and made a move to hit his brother. Alek dodged the somewhat playful attack and jogged down the hall away from them.

"You're lucky I don't feel like chasing you right now." Mirek turned to Bron, unamused.

"To be fair, we never really thought you'd agree to do them, and then it just became kind of funny to see how much we could get out of you. You do take your work very seriously, brother. After a while, we didn't have the heart to tell you to stop." Bron held the parchments in front of him like a shield.

Mirek grumbled by way of an answer.

"Where are you heading? I figured you'd be locked inside with your bride. Do you have an appointment coming into our airspace?"

"No, all my appointments are via communications devices. Is Vlad home? I have some updated orders I need to tell him about. I want to make sure we can handle it while manpower is diverted to cleaning up the mine toxins." Mirek reached over his head and stretched his sore stomach muscles. His wife might be insatiable, but he could hardly protest that she wanted him—in a variety of interesting ways and positions. "Vlad is at the mines with Kendall. Clara is here helping Alek with the ceffyls. Their new breeding program seems to be going well. Soon the far pens will be full of solarflowers and ceffyl babies."

"And the mines? How's clean up? I haven't heard anything recently," Mirek asked.

"Alek doesn't want Kendall out there so close to her end time with the pregnancy. She, of course, ignores him and goes anyway. And now that her parents are no longer gracing us with their presence, Clara will go to Mining Village to stay with Vlad. I'm not sure when she leaves. They want to have the baby there with Arianwen as midwife."

Mirek was excited for his brothers and prayed that he too would someday have a child to add to the family's good fortune. Though, after what the Medical Alliance doctors had told him, he wasn't sure if and when that would happen. Mostly, he tried not to think about it. "It makes sense that he would want to be near the village where he was born. And the miners love Lady Clara as their new protector goddess of the mines. It will be good for morale to have a village baby born after the alien invasion."

"I'm going to get these old plans to Aeron. They're not the newest version by any means, but maybe it will help her figure out what she needs to. She's been sad today and won't tell me why. I thought with Riona waking she'd be ecstatic. Though marriage is teaching me the more I think I know about women, the less I really do. I will consider this nesting and figure out a way to help her." Bron adjusted the papers in his arms. "Since it appears Riona is well, we should have a celebration. Since we had to cancel the mining festival this year with everything happening, I think the people would love the chance to meet our wives. You should also send one of the runners down to the palace to deliver the news to the king and queen. They asked about you last time I was down there to discuss possible peace treaty implications with the Var. They're worried about Riona as well and will be pleased to hear the family is finally complete."

"Good idea." Mirek nodded. "I'll send a messenger today. And I'll send word with Clara to the mines so Vlad will know about the new orders."

"I'm sure it will be fine. We should have some surplus ore left over."

Mirek didn't bother to tell the high duke that surplus often went away really fast when mining operations were stopped for long periods of time—like the months it took to clean up the mines from the Tyoe chemical dump.

Instead, Mirek said, "As to a celebration, maybe not so soon. The princesses are all pregnant, my sisters are pregnant and the new Breeding Festival is coming up in a few months. There will be much to celebrate, and finally a reason for Alek to reveal the contents and location of great-grandfather's liquor stash."

According to family legend, their great-grandfather had broken into the Var palace and stolen several bottles from the cat-shifter king's liquor storage. Alek had found where it was hidden and had lorded it over his brothers ever since, teasing them with what he claimed was a very fine bottle of Qurilixian rum.

Bron started to walk only to stop. "These are politically strange times, are they not? I think the gods waited to bless us this year on purpose to give us support and hope. We had aliens trying to take our mines. They kidnapped me and tried to poison the land in the process. It looks as if we will reach a peace settlement with the Var now that King Attor is dead." He shook his head. "Though I welcome an end to our planetary battles, I don't foresee peace lasting long. King Kirill is Attor's son, and I doubt we can ever trust a cat-shifter."

"As long as they stay on their side of the planet…" Mirek let his words trail off. He didn't really see peace lasting either. They had been warring with the Var for a very long time, so long that many didn't even know why they were fighting. Luckily, the brothers didn't see many battles being so far north. The king preferred they handle off-planet relations at the mountain fortress.

"Lady Riona, forgive me, I almost didn't see you there," Bron said, causing Mirek to turn his attention back around. "I am pleased to see you awake. I am Bron, married to your sister." He smiled at her. Riona nodded and drew her arms close to her body in a protective gesture. Bron continued, "I didn't have a chance to wish you many blessings on your marriage, but I offer them now."

Riona nodded again. "Is my sister…?" She frowned. "Is she…?"

"Are you worried about her condition? I promise you, she is healthy. The baby is well. I have ensured she has the best medical care. Alliance doctors come monthly to check all of our wives." Bron slowly continued to move away. "Have Mirek bring you by our home later. Aeron has been very anxious for you to wake up. She's been by your side almost every day and she has terrorized your doctors to figure out what was going on with you." Bron nodded at Mirek. "As has your husband. Between the two of them, I'm surprised the Medical Alliance will even agree to come back here."

When Riona merely stood not really answering him, Bron left them alone in the corridor. Riona moved toward Mirek.

"You should have just asked him what you really wanted to know," Mirek said. "You're worried you hurt Aeron's feelings."

Riona didn't meet his eyes.

"Would you like me to take you to her?" he offered. "I can show you which hall is hers, though maybe you already know? I've been meaning to ask, how did you make it outside? Most people are confused by our corridors if they don't know their way around."

"No one showed me," she said. "I got lucky the first time and have a knack for memorizing my way around new locations. Today I just followed the same path and then heard you talking. I followed the voices."

"You are very resourceful, wife." Mirek reached for her cheek. His stomach might be sore and his body drained, but if she asked it of him, he'd go to her and make love to her again—anything to please her.

"What's this about the Var?" She changed the subject. "The Galaxy Brides uploads said something about territorial skirmishes, but the way you were talking about peace treaties makes it sound like you are at war."

"We call it war because we do not get along and fight whenever our paths cross, but the fighting has been more covert as of late. They try to invade us. We defend ourselves. They try to kidnap and kill our princesses, we kill their king." Mirek motioned that Riona should walk with him. Instead of leading her deeper into the mountain fortress, he took her toward the home's entrance. The corridor led to a larger one. "While we're here, I should point out these five hallways—you know the way to our home, this center hall we came from leads to the common rooms. The first hall was Bron's, but now that he is married he took the tower rooms so you go down that hall and then take the stairs up to see your sister. Second hall is Alek and Kendall. Vlad and Clara are on the end. If you take side halls they'll lead to dead ends and mazes, so be careful."

Riona nodded.

"And this way is outside," Mirek said, before picking up the conversation where it had left off. "The Var have a new king. He claims to want peace, but we will see. Not many Draig will believe the cat-shifters capable of honor."

"So dragon-shifter and cat-shifters? Are there any other kinds on your planet?" she asked.

"Just beautiful women." He gave her a playful look, grinning.

"So cat-shifting enemies on the planet. Tyoe attacking from offworld. A plant that puts me into a coma. It doesn't seem very safe here. Especially for me, since you can add killer dragon boys with rocks to my list of worries."

"They meant no harm."

Riona rubbed her scalp. "Tell that to my head."

"You have nothing to worry about regarding the Tyoe. That threat has been taken care of."

"So I guess Aeron was wrong. We didn't really need to come here after all." Riona paused as they reached the entrance. She looked around the yard, taking in the nearby forest and open sprawl of the valley. In the mountains, the trees were skinny and tall, not like the fat round trunks of the forest near the festival grounds. Noise carried better here. The mountain home blended with nature to create what Mirek thought of as the perfect balance of convenience and beauty. The shout of a young boy sounded from the far end of the valley and she stiffened.

"The gods brought you to me," Mirek stated. In his heart he felt it to be true. To put her at ease, he tried to dismiss her fears. "As to other threats, I will give my life to protect you. Even the Var know women are special and to be protected. King Attor was a madman, but he is gone now. They won't harm you. As for the yellow, you just need to avoid the forest by the palace where it grows. If you find yourself near it, don't put your face on the ground."

RIONA EYED THE PART-REPTILIAN, part-mammal creatures locked behind the wooden bars of the stalls. "So this is a ceffyl." She glanced at Mirek. The bright sunlight from outside shone in the stable doors to frame his body. It obscured his face and distorted his figure.

"It is." He tilted his head and yelled, "Out, boy!"

Riona jolted in surprise. A young boy popped out from behind a post and kicked at the ground as he walked out of the stables, making a wide arc around her. She automatically eyed his hands for rocks. He carried none.

"Like the mines, the ceffyls are a family responsibility. Alek manages the herds and breeding. Until recently, they've only had about a fifty percent live birth rate. If we lose a herd, it is not easy to repopulate since the beasts have a three year gestation period." Mirek came next to her and lifted his hand toward the animal that had caught her attention. The animal slithered its long, narrow tongue in response. "You'll want to move slowly until they know you better."

"What happened recently?" Riona found the creature's reptilian eyes fascinating.

"Clara has a form of telepathy and can communicate with the animals. She learned why they are obsessed with solarflowers—a native plant that normally makes them sick. However, it appears they need the flower for healthy pregnancies. So far, results of the new diet had been promising. Alek raised the birthrate to about seventy-five percent in less than a year just by changing their diet."

"I know Kendall from the ship, but I don't think she likes me very much. I don't remember Clara. I'm usually very good with faces and names." Riona lifted her hand toward the beast. Apparently, she didn't do it slowly enough, because it tamped the ground with its large hooves and swung its head side-to-side while backing away from her.

"She is from Redde and did not come by way of the same ship you arrived on," Mirek answered. He slipped his hand under hers to hold it steady. The warmth of his body invaded her fingers, traveling down her arm to her side. She took a deep breath, smelling his familiar scent. Her body responded.

The ceffyl licked her fingers, ticking them. Riona pulled her hand back. "I think I can ride it."

"You want to ride it? Have you ridden creatures like this before?" Mirek stroked the animal's face.

"I'll admit, the giant horn coming out of its head is daunting, but what's a little danger?" Her heart beat in the familiar call of excitement. "Besides, when will I get another chance?"

Mirek dropped his hand. "What do you mean? There are always ceffyls here."

Riona looked at the ground before forcing herself to meet his eyes. "Mirek, I know you want to be married. I get that. Your culture is very traditional and geared toward family. There is nothing wrong with that. You have good hearts. I can see that. Any fool could see that. But this isn't my life. You said it yourself, every bride has a purpose here. Aeron is fixing communications. Clara is a ceffyl talker. Kendall is cleaning mines. I'm not really useful to onworld living. I can fly ships, but I really don't want a job as a pilot. And I doubt you have use for a professional vagabond."

"But the gods—"

"Mirek, please, listen. I really do like you. You're a good man. I see that. This is nothing you did. I think the gods sent me to bring my sister and that's it." Riona still wasn't sure she believed in gods and fate, but Mirek did with such conviction it was hard not to acknowledge the possibility. "If this is what Aeron wants, then I won't interfere. I heard your conversation with your brothers. I know he cares for Aeron. She deserves to be happy."

"And you don't?"

"What I need is not necessarily happiness." Riona thought of the fifty-thousand space credits.

The reminder sat like a weight on her chest and gathered stress in her stomach. "And my staying is not necessarily what is best for your people. Think about it. If the gods did arrange all this, then why did you not meet me when you were supposed to? By your own people's logic, we would have met during the ceremony at the right time."

He said nothing. She hated the stormy look in his eyes. There was so much passion in him, and perhaps anger or frustration, yet he held it in.

"I am not my sister. We live very different lives. You know I'm Jagranst, so you know what happened to my world."

"Aeron has told me some of the story," Mirek acknowledged. "And just the stories I've heard over the years from other dignitaries."

"An alien race called the Gregori wanted to test a weapon they'd developed. My planet was located near enough to make the trip short for them but far enough out that no one would see the blast. We were simple people. My parents were strict but loving. We obeyed our god. We had our traditions. We didn't make noise in the universe. We were just another planet of people trying to live the way we were raised to live." Riona took a deep breath.

"You don't have to tell me if you are uncomfortable with my knowing," he said.

"No, it's not that. I just have never had cause to tell this actual story. It's strange saying it out loud." She let loose a long sigh. "The weapon ship never even landed. I doubt the people on my world even knew it was coming. We didn't fight with other aliens. We didn't have special fuel ore like you do here. I was in space when it happened. We had an offworld chaperone who took us to the Zonar District for a social learning exercise my parents had signed us up for. I was so irritated that they'd made me go with my sister. Even then she was such a know-it-all and we didn't really get along. I was always in trouble and she was always lecturing me about it." Riona gave a small laugh. Some things never changed.

"You two were the sole survivors," Mirek concluded.

"Yes. The weapon detached a land drill, made a hole on the surface and then followed it with a laser blast. I suppose you could say fate got our revenge as the weapon ship was situated over an energy factory. When the factory blew, the resulting blast hit the Gregori ship. It was over in a moment. The chaperone did his best by us. Lantos made sure Aeron got into a Federation prep school, and he would show up when I called to be bailed out of some planetary detainment. I found out he died a few years after the explosion. He'd been trying to help some orphan kids and they ended up stabbing him for his trouble and his money book."

"That could not have been easy for you." Mirek tried to pull her into his arms.

The comfort would have been nice and warm and safe, but she kept back. At the moment, she felt too vulnerable. "Aeron will be a good fit here."

"And we welcome you as we do her."

"I told you that I am not proud of everything I've done, but neither am I ashamed. I am a survivor. It's all I know how to be. If I need money, I challenge someone to a game of chance. Most times they pay, sometimes they don't. When you're stuck on some fuel dock without space credit, the only acceptable way to earn is to win. If I need a ride, I work on a crew—sometimes the ships are luxury crafts, sometimes they're more piratical. When I was a lot younger and desperate, I stole food to keep from starving, but I never steal high-credit items. I never cheat. I sometimes fight. I sometimes run from the law when I get myself into a bit of trouble."

"You live honorably in a tough circumstance," he concluded.

Riona looked at him in amazement. He was so ready to believe the best in her. The confidence in her honor was strange. "And I never go back on a bet. If I lose, I pay my debts."

"Range," Mirek concluded.

"I owe him money," Riona said.

"If that is why you tell me this, then consider it done. Tell me where to send the money and I will pay this debt for you." Mirek smiled as if this took care of the problem.

"*I*," she emphasized, "owe him money."

Mirek had no idea how large her debt was. She couldn't let him pay fifty-thousand space credits on her behalf. Though, to be honest, she probably wouldn't let him pay off five space credits of her responsibility.

"Very well, but the offer stands," he stated. "As my wife, what I have is yours."

"Mirek, please understand, I don't know that I can be a wife. I honestly never thought about it." She jumped slightly as the ceffyl made a loud snort in her direction. "Right now I need to earn. This society doesn't really lend itself to my skills and I don't want to take advantage."

"So you wish to earn, and to do this you think you have to leave?"

Riona nodded.

"And your wanting to leave has nothing to do with your dislike of me?"

"Dislike you?" She shook her head. "Mirek, of course I like you. I don't think I can be married to you, but we did have fun last night, didn't we?"

"What if I gave you a job as my assistant? You come with me on ambassadorial missions. Help me greet alien dignitaries. You clearly don't have a problem traveling to space and meeting people. Besides, you were very ill. I don't think you should be doing extensive travel at this time." He lifted his hand as if he'd touch her face, only to stop and thread his hand through her arm instead to lead her out of the stables to the brightly lit yard. Wind stirred through the trees, crashing leaves together.

Riona did need to make a little start up money if she was going to join any high-stake games, and she did like Mirek. Staying with him a little longer wasn't a hardship and would actually be fun. "At a fair wage for the job."

"Naturally."

"Minus food and lodging?"

"Nonsense. You are welcome here as a guest. I won't charge you for food. We don't charge anyone for food."

She agreed to his terms with a nod. "And the marriage thing?"

"We have our traditions. As long as you remain you will be called my wife by others. I would appreciate it if you didn't try to tell people otherwise. It is a matter of honor here. Having dealt with many offworlders, I understand that not everyone thinks as we do. I will not force you to be with me. I will only pray that you come to understand as I do that the gods do not make mistakes in these matters. You were sent here for a reason, though you might not have found it yet."

Riona didn't want to argue the point. He was being fair to her. How could he have known who she was when he tried to marry her? That she wasn't there to be a wife? She came to the planet with the other brides. The mistake was forgivable.

"I have been punished for impatience once. I will not make the same mistake again."

She arched a brow, confident she didn't understand the full meaning of that statement. "So when is our first mission?"

"Possibly in a few days. I was going to try and communicate from the ground, but negotiations would go better in space."

"Few days it is. Now, enough of this serious talk." She stepped closer to him. With the heat from his body came the promise of heart-racing pleasure. "How about we find some mischief?"

"What did you have in mind?"

"Sex in the..." She glanced around. "Well, anywhere but the forest. I don't really want to wake up five years from now in an isolation chamber."

"Sex? Again?"

"Are you complaining?" She smiled sweetly at him and batted her lashes.

"Never, my lady. My body is yours to use as you will."

"Mm." She pulled at his shirt. "I like the sound of that, dragon man. Now throw me over your shoulder and cart me away."

Riona laughed as he did just that.

8

MIREK COULDN'T TAKE his eyes off his wife and she couldn't seem to keep her hands off his body. It would have been perfect but for one tiny thing—she didn't really think of herself as his wife. How could he blame her? He had failed to claim her as he should, and a small part of him worried that his failure meant they really weren't married. And, if they weren't married, how could he expect their life forces to merge. If they were really married, he'd feel her inside of him—not just his love for her, but more than that. They would join. She'd hear his call and he hers. They would feel each other's emotions. She would become a part of him, and without her he would not be whole.

Such was the way with married Draig.

Such was the way he wanted it to be with Riona.

It was not. He tried, almost fanatically, to feel her emotions as his own, but he was blocked from her. The only thing he was sure about was if she did leave him, he'd never recover. Married or not, ceremony or not, there was one thing he understood above all others—she was the only woman in all the universes for him.

Mirek loved his non-wife wife.

He wanted to tell her every time he looked at her, but he refrained. Already she had paid a steep price for his impatience, and he would not risk angering the gods again. He would earn her love first.

"Done." Riona dropped the large report on the couch next to Mirek's leg. She rubbed the bridge of her nose. "Quiz me if you want, but I'm pretty sure I can manage if these Redde aliens should visit again."

"Redde?" Mirek frowned. "No, you were supposed to read the report on the Lithorian negotiations."

"But I wanted to know about Clara's family. The way you describe them is fascinating. I've never met a Redde, and I can't imagine a people who wear hair cones on their heads and never touch their children after childbirth."

"You will meet the Redde nobles in due time. Right now, I have to focus on the Lithorians. We need to order chocolates for the upcoming Breeding Festival tents." Mirek sighed. He lifted his Redde report and tossed it away from him to make room on the couch for Riona. He patted the cushion indicating she should join him.

Riona instead leaned over the back of the couch and kissed him on the top of his head. Her lips found their way close to his ear, and she whispered, "Reports are boring. I'd rather just do, not read about it."

"Unfortunately, this is part of your training. Unless you have changed your mind about my paying off Range for you?"

Riona stiffened and stood. "I didn't ask you to pay him off. I asked for a fair wage. And you're right. I have a job and I'll do it. I'll read the report now without complaint. I earn my own way."

Mirek regretted his words, not meaning to make her feel bad. He wished she'd just let him take care of her problem, but again he reminded himself that she was not fully his wife and he had no right to insist. "I am sorry for the necessity. The Lithorians are a very tedious people and…" He sighed. "Perhaps this is not the right negotiation to take you on for your first time. I can go myself."

Riona quirked a brow. “I can handle a few monks. Don’t worry. I’ll read it. Every word.”

Mirek nodded, wishing she would come and sit by him.

Riona grabbed the Redde report and disappeared into his office. She returned with the Lithorian documents. The report was twice as big as the Redde one. “Before I get started, what do you say we go take one of those ships you say you have up into space? Just the two of us?”

“Without a pilot?” He laughed.

“I can fly,” she insisted, dropping the document and standing behind him. “Or do you have land cruisers?”

“We have ceffyls.”

“Hmm, cliff jumpers?”

“Cliff jumpers?”

“If you have to ask that probably means you don’t have them. They’re for jumping off cliffs and gliding down.” Riona sighed. “What do you have that goes fast?”

“Liquor supplies when my brothers are celebrating,” he teased.

Riona laughed. “Now there is an idea. What do you have to drink in here that is not Maiden’s Last whatever?”

“Use the food simulator,” he offered. “Maiden’s Last Breath is only used as part of the ceremony.

It's tradition. We don't serve it at any other times because it takes a long time to prepare."

"You have a food simulator?" She gasped in surprise.

"*We* have a food simulator. You live here too."

"Where?"

"Wall panel, over the table." Mirek pointed in the general direction.

Riona went to the wall and felt around. Within moments, she had the panel open and was looking at the unit. "Why didn't you say we had this? And why would you keep going to get trays of food when we can just make something to eat right here?"

"Have you tasted food simulator food? I'm sure the creators even know it tastes substandard. That is why they call it simulator and not replicator."

Riona chuckled. "I never thought about it like that. Of course, when you're in deep space and starving, you take what you can get. At least this way food doesn't spoil and doesn't taste like those tiny tubes of paste mineral supplements that were so popular before this technology came out." She began pushing buttons, barely looking at what she was doing. "Have you ever had Old Earth whiskey?"

"I don't believe so." Mirek watched her. "Do

you think that maybe you should go and see your sister? It's been two days since she visited."

Riona's hand stopped moving over the panel. "I know you're speaking out of kindness, but my relationship with my sister is none of your concern. We're not like you and your brothers."

Mirek saw the cold mask falling over her features. This was one topic she would not discuss with him. He wished he could fix it for her. But as only her lover and not a husband, he had no right to pry.

"We meet with the Lithorians tomorrow," he said.

"I know." She started pushing buttons with a renewed force.

"You will be representing this planet," he insisted.

"Fine." She tapped her fingers against the unit. The simulator made a small noise and she opened it. He expected liquor. Instead, she held a bowl of steaming food and set it on the table. She grabbed the large document off the couch, placed it next to the bowl and opened the report to the first page.

"Are you angry?" he asked, confused by the change in her.

"Just trying to do my job." Riona refused to look at him as she ate and read. She didn't say another word.

Riona read every last word of the Lithorian report—every last tedious word. Mirek's reminder that she needed to speak to Aeron had left her feeling guilty, which in turn had irritated her, which had caused her to stop speaking and focus on the report. She now knew every cultural nuance to the Lithor Republic old society. A small pain throbbed behind her right eye—every last, tedious nuance. Closing the report, she left it on the table. Her bowl was already recycled so she wasn't leaving too big of a mess behind.

Mirek had gone to bed a few hours before so she guessed it was late, though because of the planet's light she could see just fine until she reached the top of the stairs. The bedroom was dark. Riona walked in the direction of the bed. It was strange sleeping next to someone, not that they'd done much sleeping in the last few days.

Being with Mirek was one of the few things on the planet that made her heart race. It made her feel alive. She needed that rush, had since that fateful day long ago. She needed to live fully because so many could not.

Riona stopped walking as her legs hit the edge of the bed. She automatically pulled out of her clothing and dropped them on the floor. This was only temporary. Riona understood herself well enough to know she wouldn't last on such a tame planet. She survived. That's who she was and what she did. She didn't know how to be anyone else. Right now, to survive, this was her adventure.

Then why did her hands shake whenever she was near Mirek? Why did her heart flutter and her stomach tighten? Why did his opinions matter? If she was a true survivalist, she would have taken his money for her debt and been done with it. Yet, even though he offered it freely, that felt like stealing, or in the very least taking advantage of the Draig people.

"I'm not that kind of thief," she whispered, staring at the bed, trying to make out his form in the darkness and unable to.

"Riona?" Mirek mumbled sleepily.

"I finished," she said, crawling onto the bed next to him. Her wrist slid along his naked arm as she moved. Fur covers padded her knees.

Keeping his elbow on the bed, he lifted his forearm and touched her hip with the back of his hand. She stopped moving. Mirek lazily stroked her outer thigh where he could easily reach from his position on his back. That small caress held more intimacy than she was used to. She tried to dismiss the connection. Mirek was her first and only lover. He'd saved her life when she'd fallen in the yellow.

He'd tried to marry her and had a kind heart. It was only natural she'd feel connected to him. It didn't mean that the connection would last forever. It didn't mean she loved him.

Sex was just sex. Like adventure was just adventure. This was a way to make her feel something. But if she knew anything, she knew that rush of adrenaline would end. Everything eventually ended. As would this moment. It didn't matter what she wanted. She was insignificant in the whole course of the universe. Fate didn't care what it did to her. Destiny was a joke. His gods didn't exist. This moment was merely the byproduct of coincidence, an accidental meeting. She would be a fool to read more into it.

"Are you…?" He stopped moving his hand on her arm. The words were sleepy. "Are you feeling sadness?"

Riona stiffened. How could he have known that? Lying, she answered, "No, why would I be sad? That would be silly. I am actually very good right now. I have shelter, food, a job…" She pulled her arm away from his touch and flopped over on the bed. The soft covers pressed against her back. "And a warm, comfortable bed." Forcing a short laugh that held more humor than she felt inside, she added, "This beats being crammed into a tight corner of a loading dock and hoping some alien rodent doesn't gnaw off my toes in the middle of a sleep cycle."

"Oh, I thought maybe we were…" His words trailed off into a mumble she couldn't understand.

Riona, thinking to comprehend what was happening, laughed again but this time for real. "Mirek, are you sleep talking?"

"Perhaps," he mumbled. "I went there yesterday."

Unable to help herself, she said, "Is there something you needed to tell me?"

"You have really pretty hair," he answered.

"Do I now?"

"I used to brush it when you were in the isolation chamber. It was the only part of you that I could touch without making you scream. I used to worry that you were locked in pain." He readjusted next to her on the bed and sighed heavily.

"I wasn't," she assured him. "I barely remember anything from that time."

"You made my manhood sore earlier, but I liked it. Alek is jealous because my wife makes me walk funny."

Riona bit her hand to keep from laughing. This was wrong. She should either wake him or let him sleep. "I'm sorry for that." By the bounty of Jareth this was so wrong. "You like being sore?"

"We have to get the chocolate or the queen will

be mad. She'll shift all dragon on us and tear my head off." He again shifted his weight. "And the pregnant ones are running low, but they can't shift and don't run fast so I think we're safe."

"I don't know. That one looks pretty scary." She kept her comment vague on purpose to see what he would say.

Yep, she was going to be flown to planet Hades on a one-way trip.

"Who? Clara? No, she's just not very good at making expressions. She'll get better with practice."

"What about that Riona?" Riona whispered.

"Mm," Mirek made a soft noise. His words were slow and partly mumbled as he said, "My wife is lovely, even covered in blisters. I pray to the gods every day that she'll wake up. I sit with her every chance I get, but I don't think she knows me." He sighed heavily. "Her pain is my doing. I should never have claimed her like that, but I couldn't stop myself. I saw her and I instantly loved her. How can the gods punish me for my impatience when I love her so deeply?"

Riona didn't move. All laughter drained out of her. She said nothing and waited, willing Mirek to fall asleep and stop talking.

Love? He loved her?

No, it was dream talk. It didn't mean anything.

Love her?

Love?

Riona found it hard to breathe. *No, not love. Please not love. Not love. Not love.*

Fear seized hold of her. Nothing good could come of love. She remembered the explosion, the silent death of a planet from the ship's space portal. Even Lantos had died and he was as close to an adoptive father as she'd ever had.

"You don't want love," Riona whispered, hoping that whatever part of his unconscious brain she talked to would listen to her. "You want sex."

Mirek stirred more forcefully this time and sat up. "Riona? Did you just come to bed?" He sounded more aware.

"I'm sorry," she answered. "I didn't mean to wake you. I was trying to be quiet."

"Mm, no, that's all right, I'm glad you did. I was having strange dreams." Mirek chuckled. "I'm not usually such a hard sleeper, but I guess I didn't get much rest these last several months and my body is playing catch up."

His hand searched for her on the bed. Finding her naked waist, he slid her next to him. The covers blocked his hips from hers, but she easily felt the naked flesh of his stomach and chest against her. He wrapped a strong arm possessively around her. She slid her fingers up the length of it to his shoulder. There was so much strength in his muscles. His fine form excited her. She felt small and protected next to him.

And vulnerable. Very vulnerable.

Still, she didn't pull away.

Riona couldn't speak, not right at this moment. Her usually quippy remarks warred with how she truly felt. She held her breath and waited to see what he'd do next.

Mirek's hands were gentle and caressing and a little aimless in their movements. The soft whisper of his breath tickled her skin. Were these tender moments—when she allowed herself to shut up and just be—what love felt like?

He kept his hand moving, gliding the open palm over her flesh like a Ven-5 sand ray without the teeth. The subtle movements of his body somehow worked the covers down his legs. She stirred against him and closed her eyes. His internal temperature was always a few degrees hotter than hers, and she soaked in his warmth. The sensation of him wrapped her in a cocoon.

Her lips brushed his jaw and she darted her tongue out to taste him. They'd had sex several times, but never like this. Normally they came together in a windstorm of searching hands and thrusting bodies. This time was soft and comfortable. The desperation to feel stayed tempered.

Is this what love felt like?

Riona's nose burned with unshed tears. His face nuzzled her ear and he pushed her jaw aside to allow him access to her neck. Soft kisses found her skin. She trembled violently in response.

Mirek made love to her slowly. They remained on their sides, facing each other. The position gave one hand plenty of space to roam and he explored her ass and thighs. In return, Riona touched his chest, rubbing his nipples to feel them harden at the contact. That was not all that hardened. Between them, his desire grew. The smooth, hot shaft nestled into her hip. Her body answered the primitive plea with welcoming moisture.

The magnetic force that pulled her to him was undeniable. Every piece of her lived in that moment. Her toes curled along his calf as she hooked her leg over his. She drew the tips of her fingers up the indention of his spine and back down again. He sprinkled wet kisses over her neck. She shivered as he sucked gently at her flesh. Mouth open, she turned her face to his. He gave her the deep kiss she sought.

Mirek's tongue began a slow, rhythmic thrust to mimic the sex act. He rocked his hips. Riona moaned. She tried to roll him on top of her. He resisted. Instead, he lifted her leg higher before maneuvering his hips so that his cock met the slick folds of her sex. The tip entered her but was unable to slide deep.

"Turn around," Mirek whispered.

Riona refused and tried to press tighter against him. Mirek took firm hold of her and urged her to turn. When her back was to him, he drew his knees into hers to bend her legs forward. He worked his thigh between hers as he lifted her leg to open her body to him. Within moments, he was slipping inside her. The position made for slow, deep thrusts.

His hand found her breast and he skimmed his fingers over a tight nipple. The pleasure built between them until it crescendoed in a blissful eruption. Riona cried out softly as she came. A tear slipped from her eye at the rush of emotions that followed the release. She wiped it on the bedding so he wouldn't find it.

Mirek breathed hard behind her. He didn't let her go. Slipping his body out of hers, he then snuggled her against him, curling his entire length around her. It did not take long before his breathing evened and she knew he slept.

Was this what love felt like?

Riona lay awake, staring into the darkness as she counted his breaths. Fear would not let her sleep. She refused to love him. Bad things happened when she loved.

9

"I HEAR you're going up today?" Aeron came into Mirek's home unannounced.

Riona looked at her sister in surprise. She stood wrapped in a drying linen. The material clung to her damp skin and water droplets made little splats on the polished stone floor as they dripped from her hair. Mirek had left early that morning to oversee the flight plans. Riona, thankful for a little alone time, had taken advantage of the giant water bath. The tub was like a spa, constantly cleaning itself as hot water bubbled continuously inside it. However, seeing her sister, the tension began to work its way back into her shoulders and neck.

Aeron's face had rounded some with her advanced pregnancy. Instead of taking away from her beauty, it merely added to it. She looked healthy and her smiles came easier.

"Ri?" Aeron prompted.

"Oh, sorry, I'm…wet." Riona pulled the drying linen closer to her body. "Mirek was nice enough to hire me to help out. Hopefully my experience with alien cultures will be good for something."

"Hire you?" Aeron asked, with a tiny laugh. "I don't think that's what it's called when you're married. I think you mean you're helping out."

"No, I meant hired," Riona insisted. She made her way to the stairs. "I need to get dressed. You can follow me if you like."

Aeron made her way up the stairs at a slower pace. "How does that work exactly?"

"I work. He pays me." Riona tried to keep the sarcasm out of her tone, mindful of what she'd been told of the last time Aeron visited. Her sister had left crying. Not wanting to set off the emotional time bomb, she added, "I have to pay my debts somehow."

"Oh, you mean Range?" Aeron tilted her head. "Since you weren't on a gambling ship, I don't think the law will actually recognize the bet you made with Range. He didn't really lose anything by you not paying, so he acquired no personal hardship. Qurilixen doesn't recognize Federation law, so really, I wouldn't stress about paying off a pirate. If he comes here, your new family will take care of it for you."

"This is not my family," Riona said a little too quickly. She softened her tone, seeing the stunned expression on her sister's face. "You are my family, Aeron. Just you."

Tears formed in her sister's eyes.

"Oh, no, don't do that, uh…" Riona rushed to the closet and jerked a tunic off a hook. She hurried over to her sister and shoved it toward her face. "Here. Stop that. I meant to be nice to you, Aeron. I wasn't trying to make you cry."

"It was nice," Aeron cried harder. "It was the sweetest thing you've ever said to me. Yet the other thing was so sad. I want so much for you to feel like you have a family here."

Riona backed away, unsure of what to do with so many tears. She'd rather Aeron yell at her and call her names.

"Mirek worked so hard to take care of you. I didn't make it easy on him. I questioned his every move." Aeron blotted her face with the tunic. "To the Draig, questioning them is like slapping them across their honor—deeply insulting. I didn't really understand that when I did it, but I would have questioned him anyway. You're my sister. I was so worried. And he was worried." She sniffed. "And Clara came to visit you all the time. She's telepathic or empathic or, I'm not sure what they call it. Did you hear her trying to communicate with you?"

Riona made no sudden movements and slowly shook her head in denial.

"Ah, well, I think her powers work better with animals and sensing human emotions rather than actual mind communication." Aeron waved the tunic as if to dismiss that part of the conversation. "I digress. Mirek was so distraught. Bron worried about him because he was taking care of his ambassador duties and tending to you. He wasn't sleeping. And honestly, he was a bit grumpy at times. He even spoke to a couple of aliens who claimed to be able to exchange minds and bodies. It ended up being a scam, but I think he would have traded places with you if he could. Oh, wait, I wasn't supposed to know about that last one. Forget I said it."

"I am very grateful for what Mirek did for me. He is a nice man and I wish him well with his future."

"What do you mean his future? Don't you mean your future?"

"Aer, we both know I'm not the marrying and settling down type. I'm very glad you found something here. At first, I thought you were drugged or whammied, but I can see you're happy. Family life looks very good on you."

"What do you have to go back to?" Aeron asked. "Gaming and piracy? That can't be a satisfying way to live."

Riona dropped her hold on the linen and used it to pat at her wet, cold hair to stop it from dripping. She didn't really care if her sister saw her naked. "I have to get ready."

Riona disappeared into the wardrobe to find an appropriate outfit for the ambassadorial trip. Mirek's report indicated that Draig attire would suffice, so she grabbed one of the tunic gowns and pulled it over her head.

"Ri," Aeron insisted, coming around the corner to confront her.

Riona sighed. She should have known her sister would press the issue. "I don't expect you to understand, but that debt is mine to pay and I will pay it. I live by my word. Sometimes it's all I have to get by. Mirek has agreed to let me earn a little money. When I get some cash up I'll be able to buy my way into a game. It will take some time, but I'll get Range paid."

"Gambling is how you got into this problem to begin with," Aeron scolded. All emotional teary outbursts left her as she began to lecture, "I think you have a real problem."

"Why do you always insist on belittling my life?" Riona demanded. "The games I play take skill. Yes, there is minor chance involved, but mostly skill. I stay away from things that have too much risk. To tell you the truth, there's not a lot out there for single women looking for work. Would you rather I be stuck on some fuel dock, living in a room no bigger than a prison lock? Or prostituting myself in a red district? Gambling is my job. I'm good at it. It's not illegal. I don't have to take my clothes off. I get to eat most nights." Shaking her head in frustration, she pulled at her wet hair. "What do you think I was trying to do at that tournament? I was one throw away from winning. I had it, Aer, I *had* it! I'd studied each opponent's playing style in advance. I prepped for a year for that tournament. I would have won the side bet with Range. I would have won the championship pot, including a brand new ship. A new ship is as good as any home. That was my ticket out of the constant hustle that is life." The frustration poured out of her and she couldn't stop it. "I am so tired of your judgments, sister. You hid away on a Federation ship. I was out there living. You have no idea what my life has been like. I'm glad you found your happiness here. I'm glad you liked your safe, perfect life on the Federation ship. But before you dare tell me I have a problem, you'd better get your facts straight."

"I'm sorry," Aeron whispered. "I thought it was

just a game. I didn't know what that tournament meant to you."

"It's done," Riona dismissed, suddenly not wanting to talk about it. Having a family was a lot easier when they avoided conversation.

"No, it's not."

"I don't blame you," Riona said, forcing herself to calm down. "I shouldn't have bet Range. That's my fault and I'm going to deal with it. What you came to me for was more important than a game for money. These are good people. They didn't deserve being destroyed over fuel ore. I'll figure out the thing with Range. I always do."

"Mirek has money—"

"No," Riona cut her off before she could finish the thought. "I'm not taking advantage. I'll earn a fair wage. When I have a couple of thousand credits saved I'll find a ride with one of the visiting dignitary ships."

"Then you will come back? You are married."

"No, I'm not. There were some parts of the ceremony that were not completed. Mirek knows my plans."

Aeron's face fell. "But you…and he?"

Riona felt heat creeping over her face. "We, ah, yes, we did have sex, but it was just two consenting adults blowing off steam."

"I'm not sure you know what you're doing. The

Draig are not like most men. When they mate with a woman, it's for life."

"Then I guess it's a good thing we're not mated," Riona said. That trait made sense. Mirek did seem to want to settle down and have a family. The sooner she was out of his way, the sooner he could do that. The thought made her a little sick to her stomach, but she ignored it. The quicker life got back to normal, the better.

"But his crystal is gone," Aeron insisted. "I have never seen him wearing it."

"That part we did do. I broke it. But the rest didn't happen. I'm sure he can get a replacement stone." Riona hooked her sister's arm and led her out of the wardrobe.

"I don't know if that will work. I'm not sure if—"

"I really do have to get ready. Maybe we can have lunch when I get back?"

"I would like that," Aeron agreed. She grabbed Riona's arm tightly and looked her in the eyes. "I'm very happy you didn't die in the isolation chamber."

It wasn't "I love you", but it was as close to the sentiment as Aeron had ever gotten.

Riona smiled. "And I am happy you are getting the family life you deserve. Motherhood looks good on you."

"*The Sharryn*. Nice ship." Riona left Mirek at the top of the long, narrow stairwell to go toward the machine. They were high in the mountain fortress, near the top where a landing pad had been smoothed out into the stone. Large overhead doors protected the area from the elements. As in most parts of the home, small carved holes filtered in light to see. Draig men worked around the fleet of ships—some doing pre-flight system checks on the ship, others inspecting bolts and seams, still others were carting ore crates into the cargo hold. Rocks jutted out to create a corner on the far side of the room. She heard more men working beyond her eye line.

Riona lifted her hand to touch the underbelly of the ship they were to take. The smooth, cold metal caused a shiver to work up her arm. The ship was a good size, big enough to carry a decent size crew and cargo but not so big as to be forced under luxury liner flight checks. "It's a little older, but in great shape."

"The specs said it's been flying for about thirty years but it was built before that. Travelers traded it to us for ore. I half-expected someone would come looking for it, but no one ever did," Mirek said.

"You thought it was stolen?"

"The trade was strange," he admitted. "I really only agreed to get the other ship out of our sky. Since they were stranded, fuel was the only way to do it."

Seeing one of the nearby workers with a laser wrench, she motioned toward the tool. "Can I see that?"

"My lady?" the man questioned, hesitating before giving it to her. He had a kind, open face and it took Riona all of two seconds to size him up. He'd make a horrible gambler, not that he would be the type to play.

Riona took the wrench and ducked beneath the ship.

"Uh, my lady?" the man called after her.

"It is fine, Vihelm," Mirek dismissed the man. "Riona? What are you doing?"

Riona found the small access panel and used the wrench to make quick work of the plate cover. She pulled the metal back. Whistling low, she thrust her hand inside and ran her fingers over an engraving hidden behind the oxygen cylinders. She closed her eyes, concentrating as she read the seemingly random pattern of bumps.

"Checking the ship's history," she said.

"Next to the oxygen supply?" Mirek frowned, looking into the open panel at the tanks. "The ship's logs are available from inside."

"Ships are full of interesting facts, if you know where to look. Normally, it's not in the official logs." She chuckled. "You, my lord, have traded for a smuggler. The markings behind the tank identify it to other people of questionable career paths. It's how deals could be made without the interested parties being seen talking to each other. And, if you're smuggling something off a planet, you want to be able to tell which one is the correct ship in a docking lot." She reached in again. "This ship belonged to Kinny. He, uh—" she ran her hand over the symbol, "—he specialized in food simulator technology."

"How is food simulator technology worth smuggling?" Mirek wondered.

"Oh, up until about twenty-five years ago, it was a hot black-market item. People could get units, but they were expensive and those units didn't come with full recipe programs. Before they came out with the easy-to-program units, you had to have a specialty technician do it for you. I'm guessing Kinny would steal empty units, program them and then sell them. Everyone needs to eat. There was also a lot of money in the molecule pack refills needed to make the dishes. This was before technology advanced to make the cartridge inserts obsolete." Riona dropped her hand and moved to put the access panel back into place.

When she turned to him, Mirek had a strange look on his face.

Riona gave a small shrug. "I worked selling food simulators for a few months on an emporium ship. The sales staff had a lot of free time on our hands so I would read the old logs and administration action reports." She nodded to the open panel. "Feel for yourself."

Mirek stepped forward and reached behind the tanks. "What language is that?"

"Smuggler code," she answered.

Mirek helped her hold the panel as she fastened it back into place. When she was done, she tossed the wrench toward Vihelm. The man caught it easily.

"You're clear to dock," Vihelm said. "We're finishing up. Pilot is on his way."

Mirek nodded. "Shall we, my lady?"

Riona took his offered arm and let him lead her to the detachable docking plank. There was something comfortably familiar being in the interior of a ship. Metal rivets lined the narrow corridor. The hollow sound of the grates as she stepped on them echoed like a warning to the crew. Wires and pipes ran beneath the grates, completely visible and easily accessible should there be a problem.

"Is something bothering you?" Mirek stopped

walking and looked at the ground. "You're staring at your feet."

"Oh, I was following the lines." Riona gave a small laugh. "Old habit from being on ships. I worked as a line technician for a time. After seeing what can go wrong when they're not cared for properly, I just tend to check them automatically now."

"Smugglers, food simulator sales, gambler, ship crew…you have lived a very interesting life, my lady." Mirek looked beneath his feet. "I would think it would take years to become a line technician."

"I know enough to get by when I need to," she said. "Plus, I tend to remember what I read, especially tech manuals. For some reason, the diagrams just stay in my brain."

"Read? You mean uploads?"

"I mean when I physically read something. Uploads work too, but they're different. Uploads give information but not necessarily practical application. That is why they take so long to process and apply. A lot of the time, tech manuals aren't in upload form on a ship. You have to pay to use them in schools. I don't have that kind of space credit to afford classes. Besides, reading passes the long deep space hours."

"You're an amazing woman." Mirek reached to touch her face.

Riona pretended not to see the action and turned away from him to continue down the corridor. She felt guilty after what her sister had said. This man had given so much to keep her alive, and what did she give him in return? He knew she wasn't planning on staying as his wife. She hadn't lied about that. But then why did she feel so guilty about it?

It was the sleepily confessed I love you.

Riona closed her eyes and took a deep breath. She didn't want to break this man's heart. Yet she couldn't stay. It would take a long time to earn enough to pay off Range. Besides, Mirek deserved more than a survivalist gambler with giant debts. He deserved better than she could give.

Mirek sat quietly strapped into his seat, more interested in watching Riona than looking out the portal that held her attention. He'd seen the takeoff from Qurilixen many times. The turbulence stopped, but he barely noticed it anymore. The ship's engines lessened their roar and the ride became smooth.

Mirek got the impression she was sad. Yes, she smiled at him. It was a beautiful and somewhat captivating expression that drove him to distraction. It was something in her eyes when she looked at him. He sensed her leaving him before she was even gone.

Pain welled inside him, so easy to summon as it was always right there in his chest. He had no right to demand she stay. She did not acknowledge their marriage and he could not force her to. Mirek wasn't sure what protocol was on a half-ceremony. Yes, the queen had blessed the marriage, but she'd done so without all the facts. As far as he knew, no one had ever dared lie about the gods' blessing before.

In his heart, he felt she was his wife. What he felt did not matter. He'd acted on his emotions before and she paid the price. How could he act on emotions again? The ache in his chest grew so deep that he had to look away. Never had he wanted something as badly as he did Riona.

All he could do was act honorably, do his duty and help Riona to the extent that she would let him. Maybe then she would decide to stay.

He thought of the upcoming Breeding Festival. It was hard to believe nearly a year had passed since he'd met her. If he could get her to stay long enough, maybe the ceremony would be completed. Maybe she would choose him.

The idea gave him hope and he clung to it. His

impatience had cost them both dearly, but he would not make the mistake again.

"Mirek?" she asked, drawing his attention around. "You're so quiet."

"The Lithorian negotiations are very tedious," he answered. "And they won't be over today. They'll insist we send a final document to my cousin Prince Olek to look over before they'll finalize."

"I know." Riona chuckled. "I read the report."

"I warn you, this will take a long time. Just do as I explained. Stay quiet, use full titles if you have to speak, and avert your eyes to the side. I will do most of the talking."

"I think I can handle it."

Mirek nodded. "Yes, my lady, you seem very capable."

"Thank you, my lord."

"Please don't be offended if I refer to you as my wife. It will make the introductions easier." Mirek found himself holding his breath.

"It is not an issue. You already explained and I am used to the people I meet at the fortress addressing me as your wife."

"The Lithorian ship is approaching, my lord," the pilot said over the intercom. "Connection in a few minutes."

"We will go over to their ship to greet them

once the airlock is in place." Mirek stood and offered his arm. She took it. "I feel I must again apologize for how long this will be."

"You said the pregnant ladies needed chocolate. Let's get them chocolate." Riona walked with him to the entrance. The metal floor vibrated as a long column extended from the body of the ship. The Lithorians had a matching air lock and together the two ships would form a corridor. The loud whoosh of air filling the adjoining walkway created a slight breeze at their backs. Indicator lights blinked red, then yellow, and finally a safe green. Mirek reached to press the button that would open the door.

"Welcome, Lord Miroslav, Ealdorman of Draig," the Lithorian dignitary greeted as they came across.

"By the graces of the Lithorian people, I thank you, Barun Monke of the Lithor," Mirek answered, careful not to look directly at the small alien. As they crossed over into the Lithorian ship, he stepped aside. "I present my wife, Lady Riona of Draig."

"Welcome, Lady Riona of Draig," the Lithorian dignitary answered politely.

"By the graces of the Lithorian people, I thank you for allowing me on your ship, Barun Monke of the Lithor." Riona spoke quietly and kept her eyes turned toward Mirek's face. She smiled almost mischievously and winked at him. He stiffened. Watching as her eyes turned toward the alien, he started to reach out to stop her.

"And if I may, Barun Monke, with your permission?" Riona shot her hand forward, fingers rigidly pointed up.

"I would be honored, Lady Riona, and much relieved if you did," the dignitary answered.

Mirek stiffened in confusion. What was she doing? He couldn't help but look at her hand and then the alien who was suddenly making the same gesture.

"I declare a treaty of peace between the Lithorian and Draig for the entire course of our negotiations together both today and in the future." Riona kept her eyes locked to the barun and her extended limb rigid. "We find your people to have proven honor and request friendship."

"It is well you speak, Lady Riona. I accept your declaration for peace between the Draig and Lithorian for the entire course of our negotiations together both today and in the future. We find your people to have proven honor and gladly accept friendship."

Riona dropped her arm. The barun gave a small sigh. Mirek watched, confused.

"I cannot tell you what a pleasure it is to meet you, my lady," the dignitary said. He slipped his arm onto Riona's and was completely relaxed. He looked Mirek in the eye for perhaps the first time since they'd met. To Riona, he said, "We have been dealing with your people for years, and though we do respect that they formally asked that we supply them with the traditions of our people so that they may respectfully negotiate, I had hoped the formalities would not have lasted this long. My order will be very pleased that we are no longer forced to draft the long contract and then come back to receive the prince's agreement."

Riona nodded. "I think we can both agree that friendship is better than formality."

"Agreed." The barun faced Mirek. "Same amounts as last time agreeable to you then, Lord Mirek? Our chocolate for your *Galaxa-promethium* ore?"

Mirek nodded, still stunned.

"Wonderful. Next time we'll bring the delivery ship with us, but it can be here possibly by tomorrow to deliver your chocolate and pick up our shipment. Now that negotiations are over, what do you say we have a drink?" Barun Monke kept a tight hand on Riona, leading her forward. "I have a wonderful bottle of chocolate liqueur. The food simulator companies have been trying to recreate it, but they do not know our secrets."

"I tried food simulator chocolate once at a

tasting festival," Riona admitted. "They did not even come close to your quality."

The barun laughed. "They received many complaints about that failed experiment. It gave several alien species a strange bloat and humans who ate more than a bite lost their insides."

"Some things cannot be simulated," she agreed.

"I do hope you will continue on with our ambassador," the barun told Riona, before saying to Mirek, "I do enjoy your wife. She is delightful."

Mirek merely nodded, still shocked at how easy it was to get out of Lithorian tradition.

"He actually laughed," Mirek said in shock. He jostled as the ship descended onto the planet. "The barun actually made a noise that wasn't droning politeness."

Riona couldn't help chuckling. The shocked look on Mirek's face had been priceless. "For the record, that treaty is only good for Monke. You'll have to do it again if they ever send another to replace him."

"How did you know to do that?" he asked.

"How did you not know?" she answered.

"They didn't tell me I could."

"You didn't ask. From what I understand, you

had said you wanted to honor the traditions of their people. So they let you do that. But they don't require it and actually prefer the easy route. Yet who are they to deny the request if tedious is what Draig people require. They need ore for their missions and were willing to deal with your tiresome customs to get it."

"We are the tedious ones?" He shook his head in disbelief. "It only took two seconds. I dread this event all year and you finished it in two seconds. Why didn't you tell me you could do that?"

"And ruin the fun?" Riona shook her head in denial. "You looked so adorable trying to tell me how to behave."

"Adorable?" He pretended to frown.

"Sorry, I meant manly. Very, very manly," she corrected.

"You more than earned thousands of space credits with that achievement today, my lady."

"A fair wage is all I ask for." She sighed, pleased at how well she'd done.

"Prince Olek is going to be very happy he doesn't have to read those negotiations anymore. He's expecting a large contract." Mirek gave a long sigh of relief. "And I am very happy as well."

"Glad I could have a purpose." She closed her eyes as the ship jerked toward the landing pad, only to open them once they touched down.

"We're home, my lord," the pilot said over the intercom.

"Perhaps this is why the gods sent you to me," he said quietly when the engines stopped.

Riona didn't answer but found she liked the idea that she was useful.

10

LADY CLARA and Lady Kendall would not stop staring at her, Aeron would not stop grinning and their husbands seemed grateful that the wives had something entertaining to do. Riona did her best to relax, but noble dinner parties were not her thing. Up until Aeron showed up and ruined her tournament win, most of her meals had been eaten on the go.

Okay, so at least she wasn't being presented to royalty and no one expected her to wear a gown. The loose comfortable drawstring pants and tunic shirt suited her better than yards of restricting material. The men wore similar outfits while the pregnant women were in maternity dresses.

Aeron had arranged for dinner to be served in the family dining hall. The food had a rich, succulent flavor, the kind of taste that came from fresh ingredients. The brothers referred to the dining hall as intimate, but Riona estimated fifty guests would easily fit in the room. Aside from the immediate family, Cenek had joined them for the meal before returning to his ceffyl duties, stating he didn't want to leave the boys alone with the herd for too long or they'd find some sort of trouble to jump into. Riona thought that perhaps what those boys needed was some firm discipline.

After dinner, the family retired to Aeron's home to relax and talk. Riona knew Kendall from the ship. The woman hated gambling and so naturally Riona expected Kendall would not like her. By the blank expression on the woman's face, that was a fair assessment. Kendall said all the polite things, but mostly contented herself with eating off her husband's plate of fruit and snuggling into his side on Aeron's couch.

Clara's expression was masked, but the woman did at least smile in her direction. It was more emotion than Riona had expected out of a Redde noblewoman. Clara inquired about Riona's health, noted how nice her complexion had recovered and graciously accepted Riona's thanks for keeping her company while she had been unconscious. Clara's husband, Vlad, gazed adoringly at everything his wife said.

As for Bron, it was clear the man loved Aeron. He touched her belly whenever he was close enough to reach it. He kissed Aeron's head whenever his lips happened to be in the vicinity. And he whispered constantly in his wife's ear to make her blush and playfully hit his arm. Aeron was happy and she was much loved. The fact became more evident with each ticking second.

Her sister's home was what Mirek had called the tower rooms. It looked like Mirek's section of the fortress, only slightly larger and the ceiling came to a sloping point above them. Aeron would be safe here, protected by strong dragons and a mountain of stone.

Riona couldn't help the jealousy she felt when seeing the sisters-by-marriage interact. Aeron got along with the other women in a way they as birth sisters never had. The Draig wives had a bond, made stronger by content marriages and pregnant bellies. Riona could relate to none of those things. She knew very little about children and even less about marriage. Despite this, she tried her best to be cordial to everyone and hide the fact that she felt like an outsider peeking in.

"Riona, you should come and see the family portrait gallery Vlad is building for me," Clara said. "I've already convinced Kendall and Aeron to have their portraits done. I would love it if you'd let me hang yours as well. There is an artist coming after the babies are born. Coe is very fast and does all his work with paint. It only takes him six solar months to complete a portrait."

Riona glanced at Mirek, unsure how to answer. He never corrected the women when they referred to her as his wife, and by her guess Aeron was the only other person on the room who knew the truth of it.

"I'm sure she'd love that," Aeron answered for her.

Riona weakly nodded. "Yes. Thank you."

"I will only let your Coe paint me if he promises to be very kind to my post-pregnancy figure," Kendall said.

"I quite enjoy your figure now," Alek said.

"Everything is swollen," Kendall told him. "And I forgot if I have feet. They hurt so they must be there." She turned her head on his shoulder without bothering to lift it as she looked at Clara. "Do I still have feet?"

"Yes," Clara answered dutifully. "And they do not look swollen."

"You are a wonderful liar." Kendall smiled.

Riona looked at her feet and wiggled her toes.

"You will be beautiful when you're pregnant, Ri," Clara said. "May I call you Ri? I feel like I know you after how much Aeron has spoken of you."

"Call me whatever you like," Riona said, uncomfortable with the turn of the conversation.

"Quit trying to up the baby count," Kendall scolded, unintentionally saving Riona from answering. "We are not having thirty kids each to compete with your family back on Redde."

Clara pouted her lip. "Twenty-five?"

Aeron laughed and opened her mouth to answer.

Bron cut her off. "Can we show them now?" He sounded like an excited child with a new toy.

Alek and Vlad instantly stood.

"Oh," Kendall said as she was forced to standing by her husband's sudden movements. "Alek, what are you doing?"

"Come," Vlad said, reaching a hand to Clara. "We made you a surprise."

"For me?" Clara asked.

"Each of you," Alek answered.

"For you and the babies," Bron said. "In the baby garden."

"Baby garden?" Riona asked her sister, confused.

"He means nursery. Nursery, plants, baby room, garden." Aeron waved a dismissive hand.

"What did you do to the nursery, Bron? We have worked very hard to get them perfect."

The men rushed ahead.

"You each have one," Alek said proudly.

Mirek helped Aeron and Clara to their feet as his excited brothers went to the baby room. The women trailed behind their excited men. Riona held back, staying next to Mirek.

"Oh my stars," Kendall exclaimed.

"What is that?" Aeron asked. "And why is it on the floor?"

"For the nesting," Alek announced, throwing his arms to the side in a grand gesture. "To help you get ready for the baby. You have all been very, um…"

"Fluttery," Vlad supplied.

"Fluttery?" Kendall arched a brow.

"I meant crazy," Vlad corrected, "but in nice way."

"Kendall, you took away the knives," Alek offered as evidence.

"Clara, you cried over a broken plate," Vlad added.

"And you hoarded a tray of chocolate somewhere. I can't find it," Bron said.

Aeron crossed her arms over her chest. "I ate it."

"All of it?" Bron blurted in obvious surprise.

Riona almost felt bad for the men. She waited for the fists to start flying. To her surprise, the women didn't readily react. Clara covered her mouth with her hand, but Riona saw her shoulders shaking with laughter.

"Are you judging her?" Kendall demanded.

"I don't know what I said. Don't be mad. I love you," Bron said quickly to Aeron. "You're beautiful, my lady, and smart and pretty and we'll get more. Mirek, you did negotiate for more today, right? There's going to be more chocolate, right?"

Mirek chuckled and nodded. "Riona was invaluable today. She assured a quick shipment."

Bron sighed in relief. "See, don't get upset. Every need will be met."

Aeron stepped back and firmly grabbed Riona's arm. Her expression was tight as she tried not to laugh. Under her breath, she managed to say, "They made me a nest."

Curious, Aeron lifted on her toes to better see. The nursery was cutely decorated in pale greens and flourishes of gold. A rounded bed had been set up against the wall and stood only a few feet off the floor. Large cage-like bars came from above to surrounded it and keep the baby within. A lever would lift and drop the bars for easy access. Nothing was amiss in that. In fact, the bed looked very expensive. Clara turned and walked from the room toward Aeron. She was having a very hard time not laughing out loud.

Riona finally saw what the women were looking at. A giant rounded nest had been placed in the middle of the room. Instead of sticks and forest debris, the men had woven a large basket pattern to create the base. Inside, furs were piled.

"Now, we didn't want to line the nest with animal carcasses like a baldric, because I know how you like the house to smell nice," Bron explained. He knelt by his creation and lifted a fur. "So we used fur instead. But if that's not right, we can go hunting and fix it."

"Please don't put dead things in the baby's room," Aeron managed.

Bron nodded in agreement.

"But we put in a secret pocket," Alek added. He leaned down and pulled at the side. "For the chocolate. That was my idea."

"I brought the fur," Vlad inserted as he went to his wife. Clara smiled at her husband and kissed his cheek.

"And—" Alek hurried over to the other side the best he could without bothering to stand up. His knees pressed into the floor as he walked on them. "Over here is another secret compartment—" Alek reached in and pulled out a sharp blade, "—for the knives."

"Oh, look at that," Kendall said slowly rubbing her stomach in a protective gesture. "So there is."

"Now you don't have to make a stockpile up high. You will have a nest on the floor where it's safer," Alek said.

"Alek, dear," Clara said. "You can't give babies knives."

All three fathers-to-be looked confused.

"They'll hurt themselves," Clara said.

"But…" Bron frowned. "Don't you want them to be warriors? I remember my parents giving us knives."

"I'm guessing you were older," Aeron said.

"But—" Alek began.

"No," Kendall firmly stated. "No knives for the babies."

"Sword?" Vlad asked.

"No," Clara said.

"Hatchet?" Alek asked. "For throwing practice."

"Nothing sharp," Kendall decreed.

"But you like the nesting, right? We did a good job on it?" Bron gestured to the floor. "I know we don't know a lot about pregnancy, but Mirek told us that you were nesting."

"Mirek knows things," Vlad said. "And it makes sense. That's what baldric mothers do. They're protective of their young, just like you ladies."

"Mirek talks to pregnant aliens on missions," Alek added. "And Kendall, you did say not to treat you like a pregnant ceffyl about to have a baby in the field."

"You tried to feed me solarflowers," Kendall stated. "And asked if I preferred a bed or straw for the labor."

"I want to make sure everything is perfect," Alek explained.

"Do you like it?" Bron asked Aeron, still waiting for her approval.

"Yes. It is a very good nest," Aeron said. She again grabbed Riona's arm and squeezed hard. "Isn't it, Ri?"

Riona nodded and couldn't help saying, "Fit for a bird, um, baby."

"Try it," Bron urged. He pulled his wife's hand and then lifted her up into his arms. He paused long enough to kiss her before setting her down in the center of it.

"Huh," Aeron said, wiggling around in the circular bed. Her head rested on one side and her calves rested on the other, elevated by the concave design. "It's really comfortable."

"Really?" Kendall asked skeptically.

"Yes. It feels like a weight has been taken off my legs and lower back." Aeron snuggled down into the furs and sighed. She closed her eyes.

"Leave me here. I'm not getting up until this baby is born."

Bron frowned. "Brothers, we made a serious error in the design."

"How so?" Vlad asked.

"Too comfortable?" Alek guessed.

"It only fits one." Bron studied his wife as if contemplating how he was going to lay next to her.

"We need bigger," Vlad and Alek said in unison.

The husbands began discussing design plans. Aeron tugged a piece of fur over her stomach and didn't move. Kendall and Clara laughed down at her.

Riona took a small step back from the scene. Each couple painted a very perfect picture of married life, and as a whole they made a family. Mirek lightly rubbed the back of her arm. A shiver worked over her, bringing with it a wave of sadness. She did not belong in this scene. These happy, contented women were not like her. Mirek deserved to be in there with his brothers. He deserved that life. Instead, he was stuck with her. Riona didn't know how to be in a family. She wasn't sure she wanted to risk her heart like that. People would wax poetic about love and loss, but those people had never had her kind of loss. Somehow Aeron had managed to get past it. Riona didn't know how.

Everything inside Riona told her to run, to find the nearest ship and fly away to parts familiar.

The others were busy and not paying attention to her. She gave Mirek a meaningful look and then quietly made her way to the front door. The sound of debating could be heard as Bron, Alek and Vlad talked over size and structure. The discussion was punctuated by feminine laughter.

"Riona?" Mirek asked, following her out of the home into the corridor leading to the stairwell that would take them to the main level of the fortress. "Are you ill?"

"No. They're having family time. I think it was time I left," she answered. Riona began to consider staying at the fortress as she watched the family interact, but knew that she couldn't. Her personality wasn't made for onworld life. Besides, what did she know about being a part of a family?

"But you are my—" Mirek quickly corrected himself. "You're Aeron's sister. That makes you family"

"They're pregnant and happy." Riona lifted her hand in dismissal of the subject and walked faster.

"And you are sad because you read in your medical file that a side effect of the medicine is that you may not get pregnant for several years," Mirek concluded. "I did not realize seeing them like that would hurt you."

"I missed that part of the file. I was focused more on my mortality." Riona stopped almost at the bottom of the stairwell. She turned and watched as he came down. When he was a couple of steps away, she said, "I've never thought about having children. I've lived my whole life thinking pregnancy equaled a death sentence. It occurs to me that having a baby should have been a concern with what we are doing, but honestly it's the farthest thing from my mind. It's like breathing oxygen. I know about it, I know I can do it, but I am not in the habit of thinking about it."

"You think pregnancy is like breathing?"

"Necessary to the survival of a species. Yes." Riona continued down. Even she wasn't one hundred percent sure what she was talking about, she did know she wanted the conversation to end.

"I find your mind very interesting."

"Do you? You shouldn't." Riona found herself rushing again toward the front of the fortress. She knew there were side doors she could take, but she chose to keep going straight. Suddenly, she stopped and he nearly ran into her back. She stumbled a little but caught herself. She started to walk again, only to stop and face him. "I lied to you about the religious thing. I can be in tents."

He quirked a brow and looked like he might laugh.

"And I can have people write about me. I don't want them to though because I don't want my story out there. I don't want people talking about me and saying where I can be found." She took a deep breath, happy to have cleared up that little lie. "I probably know less about children than your brothers do. If I'm presented with two options, in most cases I'll take the stupidest one because it looks like more fun." In between rushed sentences, she walked a few more steps only to stop and come back to him. "I'm sassy and unpredictable and flighty and probably a little addicted to danger. I gamble. I stole fuel once. I felt really bad though so I illegally transferred space credits in the amount I took into the fueling dock's account." She frowned. "I've never told anyone that."

"Ri—" he tried to interrupt.

"I don't live my life standing in one spot," she said. "I'm always moving."

"Just make sure it's adventure calling you forward, not something behind you making you want to run away," he answered.

"I don't know if I'm running away or toward. The rush makes me feel alive. I need a rush after seeing what happened. I have to live because they cannot." Riona's breathing deepened. "It's a pathological necessity I can't seem to control."

"I understand. Your free spirit is one of the qualities I appreciate about you."

"You should probably kick me off this planet. I start fights. I run my mouth off and I don't know why. I am a mess. I owe fifty-thousand space credits to a pirate. A pirate, Mirek. Who makes bets like that, even when they should be a sure thing? No doubt he's got a bounty on me, which is why I don't want my face out there on a stupid medical case study." Riona knew she looked erratic. If she were Mirek, she'd have herself quarantined. "I shouldn't be here. I came to help Aeron because she asked, and she never asks. I should have just left like I planned, and then your life wouldn't be disrupted. But I saw your brother take her and thought the worst, so I went after her to save her. That's when I fell in the yellow stuff and ruined your life."

"You did not ruin my life," he put forth. "I chose you at the campgrounds before that moment. It is because I chose you at the wrong moment that the gods put your face in the yellow."

"What? No. I did that myself. I didn't want your brother to see me watching him." Riona finally reached the outside. The light was dimmer because of the later part of day and a rare shadow was cast down from the mountain over where she stood. "And I chose to have sex with you because I wanted to. I like to think the gods have nothing to do with what we do…naked…in bed. You should know, I *really* like sex with you, but I'm afraid it's a way for me to be with you without having to be completely exposed and vulnerable. I've been thinking about it a lot. And, well, you see I'm a survivor, and I'm not sure I can be trusted."

"Riona," he stated.

She hurried, trying to get everything she needed to say out before he could interrupt. "I'm a bad sister, and I actually care deeply for Aeron. I don't know how to be a good sister. She is better off her with Clara and Kendall than with me."

"Bad sisters do not stay behind to save their sister when they think there is trouble." He sounded reasonable.

Blast him for sounding reasonable. It made her look all the more insane.

"Riona? What is this?" Mirek tried to touch her but she didn't let him.

The cool air caused a chill to work over her. She gestured erratically and then lifted her hands helplessly to the side of her shoulders. "A marriage proposal?"

Mirek's eyes rounded in surprise.

Riona froze. Had she just said that? Her? To him? Out loud? Even stranger was the fact she didn't want to take the words back. She'd been trying to convince him why he should run far and fast from her, but instead she'd ended up…*proposing*?

She eyed him, nervously waiting to see how he'd react. What would be worse—his laughing at her or his accepting? Laughing would make the most sense, but it's not the answer she wanted.

Mirek's mouth opened but no words came out.

"See, I make no sense—" Riona began to once again fill the silence when a small laugh came from behind a jutted rock near them. She turned her head sharply to the side in time to witness a boy's ducking head. Grabbing a rock, she aimed it higher up the mountain so it wouldn't hit the child when she threw it. The loud smack was enough to get him to come out of hiding. He hopped out in dragon form to face her.

"You need to learn to be a lot quieter than that if you want to eavesdrop," Riona scolded. "Now go find that Trant kid and tell him I owe him a rock. Where I come from, you don't throw a stone unless you're ready to receive one."

"Riona," Mirek said with a note of censure in his voice. The dragon boy ran off as fast as he could.

"I'm not going to hurt a child, Mirek," she shot back.

"I know," he dismissed. "I want to talk about what you just told me."

"Forget it. I'm drunk," she lied.

"No, you're not."

Riona arched a brow. "You could have just gone with that lie like a gentleman."

"Gods' bones, woman, do you ever stop talking?"

"You're saying I should add loquacious to my list of attributes?"

"We don't have that word," Mirek said.

"It means talking a lot," Riona defined.

"I'm not really one who can judge successful marriage proposals, but I'm pretty sure listing what you feel are negative qualities about yourself is not the way to do it."

"It should be." Riona crossed her arms over her stomach. "That way you know what you're getting."

"Okay, then I work too much. I'm impatient, as proven when I claimed you instead of waiting a year as the gods clearly intended. I forget to eat when I'm busy and then get grouchy because I haven't eaten. I might have known I was wrongly encouraging my brothers to build a nest for their wives as revenge for making me write some really long reports they had no intention of reading."

"Now that's funny," Riona inserted. "They looked really proud of those nests."

"I didn't tell you, but after we made love for all those times the first night we came together, I had to go to a medical booth because my man bits were really sore."

Riona gave a small laugh. "What else are medical booths for? I won't apologize for that."

"I talk to myself."

"You also mumble talk in your sleep."

"I do?" he asked in surprise.

Riona nodded.

"When you were unconscious, I'd talk to you," he continued. "A few times, when it was really late, I would have your half of the conversation for you. You are nothing like I imagined."

"Is that good or—"

"Shush. It's my turn." Mirek held up his hand and demanded she keep quiet. He was quite handsome as the breeze rustled his hair into his eyes. Running his hands over his head, he uselessly pushed it back only to have it blow forward again. "For the record, you are a lot more contrary than I imagined, and a lot more entertaining."

Riona let her gaze drift over his handsome face.

"The doctors told me that the medicine they were trying would make conceiving impossible for several years, and may cause permanent infertility. I told them to do whatever it took to save you. I had no right to make that decision on your behalf, but the other alternative was possibly watching you wither away." Mirek's expression turned sad. "I'm selfish. I didn't want to lose you. I defied the gods to claim you and that act is the most dishonorable thing I have ever done. When I saw you, I knew I had to marry you. My crystal glowed and confirmed it. I took your choice away from you. I'm impatient, selfish and I've tarnished my honor. But if you still want me, yes to your marriage proposal."

Happiness erupted inside her and she knew she was doing what she wanted. The idea terrified her and still she didn't pull back. "So we're doing this? We're married now? We're getting married later? How does this work?"

"I'm not sure. There's the new festival coming up," he said. "I think we have to complete the ritual for it to be recognized by the gods."

"You wear a loincloth for that, right?" she asked.

"I do."

"Then I agree. We will complete the ceremony. Only we'll do it privately. No reason to create a scandal over it. I mean, you're marrying me, so I'm sure there will be plenty of scandal in your future."

She gave him a mischievous smile. "I can't believe it. We're getting married."

"Yes." He nodded, grinning. "We're getting married."

"All right, so we're doing this. We're both insane, you know that." She stepped toward him and lifted her arms to his neck. "You deserve better than me, my lord."

"You should add 'talks nonsense' to your list," he whispered. "That will be the last time you say any such thing. The gods chose you for me." He leaned in to kiss her only to stop. "And even if they hadn't chosen you, I would have."

Riona tried to reach her mouth to his and frowned when he didn't kiss her. He pressed his body tightly to hers and she felt every hard and interested inch of him.

"Wait." A pained look crossed his features. "Can we do this? The gods could be testing us again. We might have to wait until the ceremony."

"Um, I'm pretty sure the abstinence boat has already sailed." Riona wiggled against him. "If you think we're not having sex anymore, then I take my proposal back and I'll ask again two seconds before the ceremony starts."

Still, he looked unsure. She could feel he wanted her, but he was trying very hard to do the right thing. It was adorable and completely unnecessary.

"Listen, starshine, if I fall into a sex coma because the gods get mad at us, then so be it. It is a risk I am very willing to take." She held on to his shoulders and hopped up to wrap her legs around his waist. "Now, take me somewhere private so I can do some very naughty things to you. If you think you were sore last time, you have really no idea."

Mirek pressed his mouth to hers and nearly tripped over himself carrying her inside their home. He slid his hands over her b to hold her weight. Riona rubbed against him. His steps jolted their bodies together.

She breathed heavily into his ear, "Mm, hurry, Mirek. I need you."

He made an abrupt turn and pushed open a door that led to one of the outer-maze hallways. She'd poked her head in once as she'd passed by. It looked like the other corridors, only no one would have reason to be in there. Mirek kicked the door shut and eased his hold. She slid to the floor. His hands instantly found his drawstring and he pushed his pants from his hips.

Riona leaned against the wall and thrust her hips forward. He pulled the drawstring at her waist and her pants slithered down her legs in a feathery caress. Without pause, he pressed her to the wall. Hard, cool stone bit into her back. His cock brushed her stomach but tangled in the tunic shirt. Mirek thrust a hand under the material so he could palm a breast.

She gasped at the roughness in his touch. It was as if a beast had been unleashed in him. His eyes glowed with the threat of the dragon. Riona moaned, enjoying his dominant behavior. He flipped her around to face the wall. Her cheek pressed to the stone. He pushed his hands up her shirt from behind and took hold of both breasts. Mirek rocked against her ass several times.

"I can smell when you desire me," he whispered. "Do you know how hard it is to resist?"

She cried out weakly. Moisture gathered in her neglected sex, but still he didn't touch it.

"Ever since that first time I was inside you, I can think of little else." He dipped down and redirected his arousal so he could slip between her thighs. "Do you know how hard it is to be patient with a woman like you at my fingertips? Each time it gets harder not to just take you like a wild man."

"Who asked you to be patient, dragon?" she challenged. "Or are you all talk?"

Mirek growled and turned her around, keeping his body behind hers. Riona stumbled at the sudden change but he held her tight to him. She faced the long corridor. Mirek pulled down on her hips to indicate he wanted her on the floor. Riona obeyed, getting to her knees.

Mirek came up behind her and pushed her forward onto her hands. Within seconds, he had his cock shoved deep inside her. Riona cried out in surprise, liking this fevered side to him. He grabbed her hips, using them to control the pounding thrusts of his hard ride. Their skin slapped together as his hips hit her backside.

Riona braced her hands against the floor, pushing back so the force of him wouldn't slide her along the hard stone. The pleasure built like the electrical shock of a blaster. His thrusts slowed to deep, rocking circles.

"Oh, oh…" Riona climaxed, hard. Her muscles tensed, clamping down on him. He gave a loud growl and held her tight to him as he jerked inside her.

Riona gasped for breath, unable to move. Mirek pulled away before gathering her into his arms. They sat half-naked on the floor as he held her.

"I have a feeling you will make life entertaining," he whispered.

Riona gave a small laugh. "I told you everything I could think of, so you can't say I didn't warn you."

11

"RIONA, you cannot throw rocks at children," Aeron scolded, holding her stomach. She breathed hard as she ambled across the yard toward the stables.

Riona's expression didn't change as she kept her rock hand lifted and her eye on Trant. The boy stood bravely in unshifted form, ready to receive his punishment.

"Throw it," a boy yelled, laughing.

"Quiet! Or you're next," Trant ordered. The taunting boy quieted but the others who were watching Trant's punishment began to chuckle.

"A rock for a rock," Riona answered sternly.

"Ri!" Aeron yelled. She turned to Mirek. "Do something."

"His mother sent him for his punishment," Mirek said. "It's decided. I cannot interfere in a matter of honor."

"I'm not afraid of what I have coming, my lady," Trant assured Aeron. "A warrior doesn't back down. But feel free to turn away if you're too delicate."

Riona brought her hand forward as if to throw but stopped the force at the last second.

"Oh!" Aeron cried. She reached for Riona's arm. The sudden pull caused Riona to accidentally release the rock. It had been her intention to scare the boy with the idea of punishment for his action, nothing else.

Trant flinched but did not run. The rock bumped him lightly on the chest. He jerked and then looked down in shock that it hadn't been hard.

"What are you doing?" Riona scolded, reaching for the fingers biting into her arm. She tried to pry them off. "You made me throw a rock at a child."

"Oh," Aeron answered, the sound strained. She held on tighter.

"Next time you throw a rock at a lady she might not let you off so easily," Mirek told the boy.

Trant nodded. "Yes, my lord. Apologies, my lady, for thinking you were an alien. You look much prettier now that your skin has grown back."

"Ri!" Aeron demanded, clutching her arm harder still and refusing to let go.

"What? Like I really was going to throw a rock at a kid." Riona turned to face her scolding sister. "That hurts. Let go of me."

"Ri," Aeron repeated. She released her arm, bent over and started panting.

"Ri?" Riona asked.

"Ri, now, Ri," Aeron managed. She fell to her knees.

"Is she…?" Mirek asked.

"*Oh!*" Aeron yelled.

"What do we do?" Mirek looked down at the woman.

"How should I know? I don't know anything about babies." Riona answered before patting her sister lightly. "Aeron, can you stop doing that?"

Aeron answered with a growl.

"Let's carry her inside?" Riona looked at her sister and then Mirek for confirmation.

"We've seen the ceffyls have babies," Trant offered. "Do you want us to take her out to the field and get Cenek?"

Aeron made a strange crying noise and shook her head violently in denial.

"I'm taking her to the medical booth," Mirek decided. "Get Kendall and Clara and my brother and whoever else looks like they might be useful."

Aeron screeched and grabbed Mirek's arm as he tried to lift her. Riona saw her sister's fingernails digging into his flesh. He shifted into dragon form and pulled her up into his arms. Aeron still gripped him but didn't fight the embrace. He ran the pregnant woman toward the fortress entrance.

"The ceffyls never sound like that," a boy said.

"Trant, go inside and help me find Bron, Clara and Kendall." Riona gestured him toward the fortress home. Then to the other younger boys, she said, "Search the grounds and make sure the duke is not roaming around in the forest."

Eager to be of help, the young boys shifted and took to the forest like a pack of wild trainrats cutting single file through the trees. Trant hurried after Mirek and Riona watched him disappear into the fortress. She breathed hard, feeling lightheaded as she stood alone in the yard. Swaying on her feet, she whispered, "I'll be along in a moment."

MIREK GAVE Riona his hand-held unit to read in hopes of getting her to stop pacing—and almost fainting—each time her sister made a loud noise in the medical booth room. Vlad had gone back to the mines early that morning long before labor even started. Alek had taken his wife away from the commotion to relax as she was feeling a little ill. Bron and Clara were helping Aeron along with one of the Draig men who had some medical training in midwifery.

"That can't be right," Riona said as her sister screeched. "Is your medical booth broken?"

"Everything is fine," Mirek assured her.

"Then why did Aeron kick me out?" Riona demanded.

"Because you, my beautiful bride, nearly fainted again," he answered calmly.

"I'm going back in."

"It is curious that Bron is in there. Traditionally, fathers are kicked out of the delivery room." Mirek thought it funny his brother refused to leave his wife's side.

"I think I can take Bron. He can't stop me from helping my sister." Riona made a move to go inside only to stop as she heard another groan. "Did I ever say thank you for giving me that medicine?"

Mirek hid his frown. If his wife was unable to give him children, he would love her regardless. That was not in question. However, if she didn't want his children, that stung a little. Then hearing Aeron call her husband a dragon beast, he imagined he could understand Riona's feelings at the moment. Childbirth did not sound pleasant.

Clara stepped out of the room. "This is why my

people have babies in stasis. Your sister is refusing medical help. She got it into her head to have the baby naturally. Everything looks good. The medical booth is right there if anything happens. Don't worry, I have nineteen sisters and eleven sisters-by-marriage back home. The topic of pregnancy and labor has come up many times in my lessons. Everything looks good."

Riona merely nodded. Clara disappeared back inside.

"Is Aeron insane?" Riona relaxed a little and looked down at the hand-held she carried. "What's this?"

"We have a new negotiation recommended by people we've been doing business with for a while," Mirek said. "I had an introduction message left last night and apparently they'll be in our airspace this evening. I'm not really pleased with the short time-line, but it could be a large order. Before I decide, I want your opinion on it. Their negotiation request seems out of the ordinary to me." He glanced at the birthing room door. "I'm sorry to do this now, but I thought it might take your mind off—"

"No, it's fine. What species are they?"

"G'am," he said. "I've never heard of them. I hoped maybe you had. There was information about their negotiations etiquette, but honestly, I have never heard of a Frendle's Chips exchange before. From what I can reason, it's a game they play and whoever wins gets to set the terms of negotiation."

Riona smiled.

"You've heard of it?"

"The G'am, vaguely. They're pretty territorial from what I can remember and don't leave their airspace too often. Mostly, I've heard stories of how they love games of chance. It has something to do with their religion and fate and taking destiny into their own tentacles—a let-the-best-alien-win kind of mentality. On the plus side, if they lose, they'll honor the bet." Riona sat on the floor and pressed her back to the wall to look at the file he'd given her.

"And what about the chips?" Mirek hid his smile, having adequately distracted his bride's mind from labor.

"Frendle's Chips? Oh, yes. I know that game very well."

"Can you teach it to me?"

Riona bit her lip and looked up at him. "Not by tonight. We don't have a board. That's probably why they picked this game to negotiate on. They hoped the short notice would give them an advantage." She flipped through the screens. "What they don't know is that you happen to be engaged to an expert. Many of my meals came from winning this game." She stopped scrolling and read. Focusing on the stipulations laid out in the proposal more than talking, she asked, "Does it say the terms in here? What are they offering?"

"Half-price ore versus double-price," he said. "The order is sizable."

"So what's the risk for you? If you lose will it put hardship on the planet?" Riona arched a brow.

"Hardship, no. Loss, yes. There would be risk."

"Oh." She handed the unit up to him. "Then maybe you should tell them no."

"It could be a good account. I really wish they'd agree to pay normal price. We don't need double for it." Mirek eyed her thoughtfully. "You know, you did very well with the Lithorians."

"And I was very happy to help."

"You also know how to play this Frendle game." He sat on the floor next to her. The birthing sounds lessened and he was glad for it.

Clara stuck her head out of the room. "All is well. We made her get into the booth and gave her something to relax."

"Finally," Riona said. "Thank you."

Clara nodded and disappeared back inside.

"I knew Aeron was stubborn, but this was crazy," she said. "Medical booths are perfectly safe.

There was no reason for her to be all primeval about it."

"You're changing the conversation," Mirek said. "Will you help me negotiate this deal? If you say you're good at the game, then you're good. Plus, I think this is why the gods brought you here. You wanted a purpose."

"I thought the gods brought me here to be with you," she teased.

"Mm, definitely that." He leaned over and kissed her, loving how relaxed she was around him. Every part of him wanted to pull her into his arms and never let go. The fact that she accepted him and wanted to finish the marriage ceremony with him made his heart soar. "Negotiation help is a bonus. And I was thinking, if you win, you should take the extra money and pay off your debt. We don't expect double and you would have earned it. Think of it as a sales commission."

He could see the denial forming on her face. Before she could say anything, he kissed her mouth hard. A small moan escaped her. When she melted into him and reached to touch his face, he pulled back.

"Tell me yes," he whispered.

"Mm, yes," she answered, leaning to continue the kiss.

He pulled back. "Good. Then it's settled. You'll do it."

"What?" She blinked rapidly in surprise. "No, I said yes to the kiss, not—"

"Too late. You can't take it back. You said yes." Mirek took the hand-held and pushed a series of buttons. "And I just sent our confirmation to the G'am. We'll leave as soon as your sister is taken care of to your satisfaction, my bride."

"But…"

The sound of a baby crying interrupted. Mirek hopped excitedly to his feet and reached to help her up. They both rushed to the door to see the newborn.

"My son!" Bron announced, holding the baby in his hands.

Mirek looked at the tiny bundle. He had dark brown hair and eyes like his father. "A fine son."

"Aeron?" Riona asked, checking on her sister.

Aeron opened her eyes and smiled. "We're going to name him Lantos after the man who saved us. That way he'll protect others who need it."

Riona nodded. "That's a good name. Well chosen."

Aeron closed her eyes.

Riona moved to look at the baby. "He's adorable, Bron. Congratulations."

"Would you carry him to our home?" Bron

asked. "I want to take my wife to her bed so she can rest."

"Oh." Riona gasped lightly as he placed the baby in her arms. A little stiff, she waited for the baby to settle. Mirck watched the scene with joy in his heart. This is what mattered in life. Family.

12

The G'am were willowy creatures, nearly transparent in their skinny white-tinted mass. The ship's interior lights reflected through their bodies when they walked by them, accentuating the seemingly random pattern of veins beneath their skin. Tiny round organs pulsated in time with each other as they traveled slowly through the blood vessels. Since they did not wear clothing, it was hard not to stare at the hypnotic pulsing of their insides.

They walked like humans on two legs, but that's where many of the similarities ended. Long, thin tentacles wiggled out from four oval hands at the end of four cylindrical arms, opening and closing like restless fingers. Riona held out her hand to mimic their greeting. Their tentacles glanced over her wrist like tiny kisses and left behind round pink marks, not unlike when her husband sucked on her skin a little too hard during love play. Only with the G'am, there was nothing sexual in the contact, just a strangely fascinating suctioning of skin.

The presumed leader stood before three others. A round eye moved a little too freely in a bald head, as if floating on the surface. However, when the creature spoke, his star language was flawless. "You accept the game?"

"Frendle's Chips," Riona said. "Territory rules."

She wasn't sure, but she thought she saw the tiny mouth smile. The creature's pulse lights quickened. "Territory rules. The game is won when it is finished."

Riona's heartbeat sped at the challenge she sensed in him. She looked at Mirek to be sure this is what he wanted.

He nodded once. "Yes. We accept the game."

"You accept the terms," the G'am asked.

"I win, you pay double. You win, you pay half," Riona said, knowing she had to lay out the agreement or risk them slipping in new terms.

Again, the G'am seemed to smile. "Yes."

"Then we accept the terms." Riona waited for their instructions. Her stomach knotted. This wasn't like when she played for herself. She felt the responsibility of an entire people's economy on her shoulders. Not to mention her personal debt. Mirek placed a hand on her shoulder and her nerves instantly calmed.

"I am Eeve, Chancellor. This—" the G'am leader motioned for one of the other aliens to step forward, "—is Teev, Champion."

"I am Mirek, Ambassador. This—" he nodded at Riona, "—is Riona, Champion."

Eeve nodded in acceptance. The group of G'am glided through their ship. Riona let the back of her hand brush against Mirek's arm softly as they walked. The vessel wasn't spectacular in any way—a medium-size cruiser of sturdy design and typical mass-production layout that made navigating the corridors easy.

Riona followed them to what was normally the commons area. The G'am had removed all traces of comfortable furniture and humanoid dining function. In the center of the barren space was a single table with a deactivated game board and two metal stools.

Teev took a seat and his floating eye moved to look at her without his having to move his head. Riona gave Mirek a small smile and went to take her place across from the alien. Teev waved a tentacle hand over the table to activate it. Metal discs lifted up into a laser game grid. Electricity snapped in slow succession. As the game progressed the electrical charges would become more intense and increase in frequency.

"We will discuss transport and delivery," Eeve said. He motioned that Mirek should leave.

"But—" Riona stood.

"We will come back for the results," Eeve dismissed.

Mirek looked at her questioningly. She nodded reassuringly at him and again sat. Riona felt more than saw Mirek leave and she missed his comforting presence. With his absence came the nerves, and she took a deep breath to steady them.

The first move was Teev's, as he was from the host ship. He took it, fast and easy. Riona concentrated on the electricity and swiped her finger to take a disc. Once out of the grid, it became inert. She placed it in front of her. The key was to work into the middle of the grid to take as many of the deep discs as she could so when the second half of the game started the outside ring of discs would be easier to dislodge.

It only took a few moves for her to realize that human hands were at a disadvantage when it came to the G'am. Teev extended a finger and suctioned the disc back with lightning speed. Still, Riona managed to keep up and they both played a perfect first round.

As she placed her last inert disc on the table in

front of her, the electricity became more frantic. Though there was no rule against finger sweeps at this level, her hand would no longer fit between the electrical snaps in the grid. She'd have to throw her discs and dislodge the rest of her game pieces.

The quiet room was not her usual atmosphere. Normally, she played in a noisy bar filled with smoke and liquor. And Teev was hardly her average opponent. He didn't speak, didn't trade barbs or try to intimidate her. Instead, he simply played with his abnormally long suction fingers that stretched thin.

This is why Riona normally vetted her competitors before a tournament. She should have known the G'am would have an advantage of some sort.

She waited for him to begin the second round. Instead, he kept his hands down and said, "Frendle's rule. I call a change."

Riona frowned. It wasn't against the rules, but it was highly irregular. "Change? What change?"

"Hello, lovely," a voice said behind her.

Riona stiffened. She didn't move.

"What? No greeting for an old friend?" Range's breath hit her ear as he leaned over her shoulder from behind. Whispering, he added, "You didn't really think you could hide from me forever, did you?"

"Me?" she shot with fake innocence. "Who said I was hiding?"

Range stood. He came to stand by Teev. The G'am nodded and stood, giving Range his seat. The pirate picked up a disc and fingered it. "You are a very hard woman to track down. I have to give you credit. I didn't expect you'd hide out on such a primitive planet. A fuel mine, Ri? Really?"

"It has its charms." To hide her nerves, she took a disc and tapped her fingernail against it. She worried about Mirek. He didn't know this was a trap. "I happen to like digging in the ground. I'll make you a hole you can crawl into." She made a show of looking round. "Where's Joner? I didn't think you went anywhere without your boyfriend? Or did you call him your bodyguard? I can't remember. You two always looked a little too cozy together."

"That's adorable," Range answered. "The way Joner tells it, you two were the cozy ones."

Riona stiffened but refrained from reacting to the barb.

"I knew it was only a matter of time until one of your old contacts found you. Imagine my surprise when it was a Fajerkin who reported seeing you with an ore mine ambassador on some primitive planet. Very careless of you, but then maybe you were just tired of hiding. I hear that happens to fugitives."

"I'm hardly a fugitive."

"Tell that to the Fajerkin. They want you almost as badly as I do." Range chuckled. His hair stood in its usual black spikes and he pulled up on them needlessly to make sure they were in place. "Tell me, however did you manage to get Torgan to initiate protocols for a possible toxic contaminate as you left Madaga? Now there is a trick I'd pay money to learn."

"Don't know what you're talking about," Riona lied. "Maybe they just got whiff of your hair cologne."

"The ladies don't mind it." When he smiled, the dark green facial tattoo along one cheekbone shifted. "But you wouldn't know anything about that, would you?" He pointed downward and whispered, "You're not all woman, are you?"

"Because I resisted you?" She arched a brow. "Since when do you play with G'am? You do know when I win, I'm not leaving with you. They won't be happy that their stand-in champion loses a fuel deal."

"I knew you'd remember my story about the G'am. All gamblers do." Range watched her through the electrical snaps of the grid. "What you didn't know is that Eeve and I are very, very old friends. When I promised him a bit of honor with his gods for reclaiming a gambler who welched on a bet, he was only too happy to lure you out of hiding. This capture will ensure good standing with their gods for the entire crew. I knew you couldn't resist Frendle's Chips and such a large winning pot. Once a gambler, always a gambler. I set the trap and you ran right into it."

"Throw your piece," Riona demanded.

"This?" He held up the inert disc and laughed. Range focused on the board. Then, swinging his arm, he crashed through the grid.

Riona gasped at the unexpected move and jumped up from her stool. Discs fizzled into dust. The game was over. She breathed hard. If they didn't finish the game, she couldn't win. If she didn't win, she didn't have the money to pay him. She looked at Teev, wondering if he would protest. He didn't move.

"The game is won when it is finished," Teev said, confirming her fears. "The game cannot be finished."

"The G'am are very sneaky, are they not?" Range loomed toward her. She stumbled away from the table, not turning her back to him as she kept distance between them. "They have no interest in fuel ore. So there will be no deal."

Riona tried to remain calm, but her body

began to shake in fear. There was nowhere to run. This was an alien ship. Teev stood between her and the exit. Mirek was somewhere onboard so even if she could get to freedom, she wouldn't leave him behind.

"Fine. You captured me. What about the one I was with?" She crossed her arms over her chest.

Range nodded at Teev. The alien stepped aside and motioned over a door sensor. It opened and Mirek was dragged inside. He moaned and they dropped him to his knees on the metal floor.

Her heart beat hard. Fear made it difficult to breathe. "He owes you nothing. He's just a pawn I was using to get your money. Send him home."

Range knelt close to Mirek and grabbed his jaw to lift his weak head. Green eyes rolled before settling on the pirate's face, glassy from whatever drug they'd dosed him with.

"Did you know when I first found this one, she was near dead, starving," Range said. "Two fat little kids were right there, so easy to overtake, chomping on a feast of stale bread and stolen meat. All Riona had to do was take it, but she wouldn't. That's her problem."

"I wasn't near dead." Riona tried not to let her concern for Mirek show. It was hard. She wanted nothing more than to run to him and protect him from danger. Inside, her very being strained to comfort him. She forced her feelings away from the surface and kept a disinterested pose. "I stood up to you just fine."

Range ignored her, shaking Mirek's jaw when the man's eyes began to drift closed. The pirate forced him to once more meet his gaze. "Do you know what she said when I asked her why she didn't take the easy food?" He glanced up at Riona and arched a brow, prompting her to speak.

"I'm not that kind of thief," she said through tight lips.

The pirate laughed. "As if a thief isn't a thief."

"Enough. Put him back on his ship. I know when I'm defeated." She sighed, trying very hard to feign boredom. "You're right. I'm tired of primitives."

Range dropped Mirek's head. "Now, Ri, *tsk-tsk*, is that any way to talk about your husband?"

Riona stiffened.

"The Fajerkin told me congratulations are in order. Though, that's not exactly how they worded it when they told me where to find you."

"Stop." Riona covered her ears. "If all this talking is your idea of torture, it's working. Just do whatever it is you're going to do to me."

He glared at her. "You wouldn't take food from children, but you'll steal from me? You are more worried about children than what I would do to you? Did you really think hiding out here in the middle of nothing would make you safe?"

He wasn't getting fear and begging from her, and it was making him very angry.

"Did you think he could protect you?" Range pointed at Mirek.

"And did you think I would come here if I didn't have an angle to play?" Riona demanded. She gave a cold laugh. "Do you understand what kind of planet he's from? Do you know what he mines?"

Range's confused look was answer enough.

"*Galaxa-promethium*, or since you probably missed that little chemistry lesson in pirate school, it's the good stuff. The premium grade." She shook her head. "His planet is full of it and his family owns it."

Range looked at Mirek in shock.

"Yeah, he's loaded." Riona nodded. "And this little heist kidnapping you're trying to stage right now is ruining a score bigger than you could have ever dreamed of. I was going to give you your fifty plus interest. Now, you get G'am honor and a broke captive. Congratulations, Range," she drawled sarcastically, "good pirating, as always. Another small time score to add to your collection of small time—"

Range backhanded her across the face, sending

her spinning to the side. Before she could stop the dizziness in her head, she heard a growl. She drew her hand to her bleeding mouth and turned to see Mirek fully shifted. His taloned fingers wrapped over what would have been the G'am throat to hold him back. Teev's suctioning fingers pulled at the protective shell of Mirek's hardened skin. Tiny threads of brown filtered into the tentacles and up the creature's arm.

"A shifter?" Range gasped. He took a step back from the fierce dragon man before them. His gaze darted around the sparsely decorated room. Mirek blocked the only escape. He reached for his belt, but like most ships, this one's protocol had been to take weapons. No one wanted a crewmen suffering from space fever to try to shoot their way out.

"Did your Fajerkin friends forget to tell you everything?" Riona laughed darkly as she pushed herself off the floor. Relief filled her to see Mirek upright. His yellowed eyes glowed fiercely and she knew he'd be capable of slaughtering the whole crew. She watched him and felt his anger curling into her body. It was more profound than anything she'd ever experienced, an invasion into her soul that she didn't want to stop. Her heart quickened. She took a deep breath.

"Let him go," Range demanded. "We dislodged from your ship. There's no escape."

"No," Riona said. "You didn't. I would have felt the tremor, and you know it."

He glared at her. "That doesn't change the fact that you owe me."

"Then fight honorably," Teev said, his voice not strained even as Mirek held him back. "Finish the game. If she wins, we honor the terms of the original agreement and pay double to the Draig in return for our release of any obligation regarding this incident. Range, her debt to you will be cleared without payment and they will be free to go. If she loses, they give us the ore for free in return for the ambassador's safe return to his people. Range, you will take the champion and her debt to you will stand."

Either way Mirek would be safe. Riona nodded. "I accept those terms on the condition that there is no changing the rules. This game is played out to the end, no changes allowed. These terms are set." She looked at Range. "A forfeit equals a win for the other player."

"No," Mirek growled, his voice gruff. His arm flexed as he lifted the G'am off the floor.

"No," Range repeated, louder. "I don't agree to that. She's mine."

"I'll pay her debt and our deal is off. We're leaving." Mirek tightened his hold on the creature.

"The terms have been accepted," Teev stated, still unconcerned with his position.

The tentacles against Mirek's arm grew darker. Her dragon man's shifted arm weakened and he was forced to let go. Cradling the limb, Mirek shook his head in denial. "Don't do this, Riona. The risk is too great."

"Take your seat, Range. Fate will be decided by chance." Teev moved to stand. The darkness inside his tentacles formed a cloudy haze inside his body.

"You planned this, didn't you," Riona shot accusingly.

Again, the ghost of a smile traced Teev's mouth. "There is reward in taking chances. I saw the opportunity to get more and I took it."

"You said you don't care about fuel ore," Range argued.

"We don't. But others do. It will make for a great game incentive." Teev's arms were down at his side.

"I don't have to play. I don't agree to the terms," Range said.

"When you boarded our ship you agreed to follow its rules. As a member of this ship, you are bound by the game terms I have set forth. If you refuse, you will no longer be welcome on this ship." The creature's eyes floated to indicate the direction of the small portal window and nothing but inky space beyond.

Range swallowed as he got the meaning. Either he play or he immediately left the ship for the deep black without a spacesuit. He took his seat and angrily waved his hand over the board to activate a new game. The gaming grid reappeared with new discs.

"Riona, don't," Mirek whispered, stepping in front of her to keep her from sitting.

She lightly touched his chest. "It's my fault for not laying out the terms of the original game more clearly. It is my fault Range is here. If I play, you get to go home no matter what happens. There is no choice, Mirek. If I play, you are safe. The rest doesn't matter. But I will be sorry if I lose your ore."

"I don't care about the ore. You're mine. You are coming home with me," he stated.

"Then pray to your gods that I win." Riona lifted up on her toes. She felt him inside her, his fear and fierce passion. This dragon man would die for her, but she couldn't let that happen. She pressed her cheek to his and whispered, "I feel you, Mirek. Whatever happens, know that I will always feel you."

"Your move," Range demanded angrily. He

looked like a petulant child with pouted lips and angry eyes.

Riona sat and tried to concentrate on the game. The deepening connection she felt to Mirek gave her strength, but it also distracted her with the fear of what she stood to lose.

Her game was not as strong as it had been against Teev, but she managed to stay relatively close to Range in score, though he was a few points ahead at the end of the first round. Her fingers shook and a few times she was zapped with electricity. The jolt stung, but nothing like the second round. Tiny burns crisscrossed over the backs of her fingers. Each time she jumped, she felt Mirek behind her ready to interfere.

As the second round started, she closed her eyes and took a deep breath, willing Mirek to relax. Almost instantly, she felt calm. She looked up at him questioningly. Had he really felt her request?

He took a deep breath and nodded. Riona felt a weight being lifted from inside her chest. Her focus returned. Range tossed his disc. A sliver of electricity shaved the side. It floated a few centimeters and then dissolved.

"No!" Range yelled, leaping out of his chair. "That was in. I get the point."

"The board doesn't lie," Riona said calmly, just to irritate him. She knew how much he hated to be mocked. "Maybe you're just not good at the game."

He pointed at her and hissed his breath through clenched teeth. Then slowly took his seat, running his fingers through his hair. "Your move, Ri."

She stared at the grid, tapping her finger thoughtfully as she made out a pattern in the seemingly random strikes. When she learned the rhythm, she was able to throw with confidence. Her disc knocked an active one off the grid.

"Stop tapping," Range muttered.

Riona would have sworn she felt Mirek touching her, but when she looked at her shoulder he stood a couple of paces away with his arms over his chest. He stared at Teev in warning. Teev seemed unconcerned and focused on the gaming table.

"Go," Range demanded.

Riona picked up an inert disc and smiled. She pretended to be bored as she again tapped the rhythm. What players like Range didn't seem to get was that gambling wasn't really about the game. It was about the players. Men like Range were easy to read because he liked being in control and he didn't like to lose. Already, he was mad about being forced to sit at the gaming table. He was the type that liked to place bets on others and then beat them with a pipe if they lost.

They played several moves before Range was zapped again. He glared at the grid and then Teev. "You know, I think you laid bad odds, G'am."

Riona arched a brow.

Range lifted the remainder of his discs and tossed them onto the board at once. They crashed and fizzled, forfeiting the game. Teev made a loud screeching noise. Riona covered her ears and flinched. Range stretched his hands behind his head and laughed.

"I don't like having my hand forced," Range said when the screeching stopped. "You should have taken that into account when you double-crossed me and agreed to this game."

Riona held her disc, stunned that it was over.

Range turned his attention to her. "As for you, I get pleasure out of knowing I ruined your big score. We're even." He leaned over and whispered. "Look at your shifter's angry face. Think of me when he's punishing you for your deceit."

"The terms are set. We will wire your space credits immediately and send a ship to pick up our ore." Teev moved to the door.

"Oh, cheer up, Teev. The gods of chance are smiling at the games today, aren't they?" Range mocked.

"Let's get out of here," Mirek said. He helped Riona to her feet and kept her by his side. She felt the tension rolling through him. They cautiously followed Range and the alien back through the corridor to the exit. When they arrived at the corridor joining the G'am and Draig ships, Riona was careful not to turn her back toward the pirate and his alien friend.

Range eyed Mirek's hold on her and realization of her situation dawned in his expression. He looked at Mirek's face and then hers. "Now that I think about it, what do you want to stay here for? Your debt is cleared. Come with me. Join my crew. Let's go have some fun."

She didn't trust him or his offer, but even if she did, she had no desire to fly away with him. "Sorry, Range, you're not my kind of pirate."

"Are you sure? I'm betting there is something we can place a wager on." He smiled, a deceptive look that hid the almost desperate need in his eyes for something to happen.

Riona felt a little sorry for him, for she'd been like him in some ways. She'd been trapped in her life, endlessly searching the universes for answers to questions she didn't know to ask. Whether it was luck, chance, fate or the gods, she'd found the answer she needed. Mirek. He was home. He was family. He was her life.

"When you find yourself in prison, don't think of me," Riona said. "And I will never think of you."

Range smirked and gave her a quick nod. Then, frowning at Teev, he grumbled, "You owe me fifty-thousand space credits."

"Is that a challenge?" the G'am asked.

"Let's get off this ship before they change their mind." Mirek took her by the arm and practically ran with her through the air-lock corridor joining the ships. He punched in his access code and barely waited for the door to slide past before pulling her through the narrow crack. Not letting the door open fully, he ordered it to close and detached the corridor. He stood, holding her tightly to his body as the ships unhooked.

"Get us out of here," Mirek demanded over the intercom. "Now."

"Please be seated," the pilot answered.

"Now," Mirek yelled. The ship lurched. He held on to her with one hand and a metal bar with the other while bracing their weight against the violently shaking motions of sudden flight. "The Fajerkin made this happen?"

Riona nodded, gripping him so she didn't fall. "Yes. They told Range. I knew he'd have bounties out on me."

"I'm cancelling their order. We will no longer do business with them. No one attacks my wife."

"Mirek, it's all right. We're safe," she assured

him. "I don't want you hurting the business because of me."

"I was thinking of breaking ties with them ever since you told me how they treat their women," he admitted. "Their business is no loss to us."

"I love you, you know it. You're a good man, Mirek." She gasped as the ship unexpectedly changed course and began to vibrate.

"You are never allowed to gamble with your life again, my love," he growled and strengthened his hold. "It is no longer yours to do with as you please."

"Excuse me?" Riona pushed against his chest and he loosened his embrace. Though still in flight, the ride smoothed. He still held on to her as he walked her down the corridor toward their seats so they could prepare for their decent onto Qurilixen.

"You said you felt it. You're inside me, Riona. I can't live without you. The ceremony doesn't matter. I realized we don't need the formalities to be together. You *are* my wife. I don't know if we were foolish or in denial, or if the gods simply decided we'd finally earned it, but you are mine and I am yours. My life is no longer my own. All that I am is yours. And all I ask for in return is you."

She forced him to stop walking and jerked him to her. Lifting up on her toes, she grinned. "Well, dragon man, if you put it that way…" Riona kissed him hard and didn't intend to stop.

"The alien craft has left our airspace. It is safe to go to your seat, my lord," the pilot's voice said. He paused. When Mirek didn't answer, he insisted, "Um, my lord? I can't land until you're seated."

Mirek leaned to press the intercom button. "Take us around the planet a couple times. I'm busy kissing my wife."

"Yes, my lord." The pilot's tone held a trace of laughter. "Orbiting the planet now."

Riona leaned to the intercom and pressed the button. Smiling seductively at her husband, she said, "Pilot, you'd better make it three times."

13

EPILOGUE - BREEDING FESTIVAL GROUNDS, DRAIG PALACE, PLANET OF QURILIXEN

"No children? Are you sure? Can nothing be done?" Prince Ualan gave his cousin a sad look. The Draig princes and noblemen watched the tents being raised for the upcoming festival. Their wives and children were inside the palace waiting for them. It was believed their eight blessed marriages would bring luck to those who searched this night, and so the princes and noblemen went to honor the prospective grooms with their presence. After the brides landed, they would slip away to join their family.

"For now," Mirek answered. He wanted children, but he was willing to trust the gods would bless him if and when it was time. "But my wife is awake and healthy. For that blessing, I would give her the medication a thousand times. If it is not meant to be, we will take in an orphan." He looked at his adopted brother and grinned. "Welcoming Vlad into the family turned out all right."

Vlad winked at him. "The House of Draig needed a little wild blood in it."

"And if none of that happens, I will have my nephews and my little cousins." Mirek smiled. Nothing could dampen his spirits. Riona was his life and he was hers. That would be more than enough blessing.

"I, for one, am just glad I do not have to don the loincloth again," Bron said. "I would not have survived another failed attempt."

"But waiting for your bride was worth it," Prince Zoran stated. He stood with his arms crossed, looking at the valley as if he was a general overseeing his army encampment.

"Yes," Bron agreed. "More than I can express with words."

"I, for one, am very pleased I don't have to read any more Lithorian documents," Prince Olek said. The Royal Ambassador had thanked Mirek profusely when he'd found out the happy news.

"Oh?" Prince Yusef inquired. "Please don't tell me we're no longer getting chocolate. My firebird won't be happy."

"Do not worry. Princess Olena will be well stocked. Lady Riona renegotiated the deal. We get all the chocolate we want, whenever we want," Olek said. "All we have to do is place the order."

"Well done, Lady Riona," Ualan stated, nodding happily. "This will please the women greatly."

Mirek watched as a group of loin-clothed men walked through the grounds. He could see their excitement in their steps. Soon that energy would be pulsing through the air as dusk came to the planet. The small thrill of anticipation filled him as he thought of what was to come. Though not necessary for their marriage, his wife had insisted he bring the loincloth with him. Apparently, she had her own night in a tent planned and for them there would be no restriction on what could happen.

"I almost feel sorry for them," Mirek stated, nodding at the grooms. If they found brides, they would not be able to claim them completely until the ceremony was finished. "If they're blessed, they're in for a very torturous night."

"After the problems with the last shipment, we almost cancelled our business with Galaxy Brides, but then we'd deny all these men the chance at the happiness we have found. I may not like how they do business, but who are we to question how the gods deliver our fates?" Ualan motioned the others to follow him down into the valley. "Come, let us find the rum and make a toast to our hearts. Without our wives, our lives would not be whole."

"I can't explain it," Riona told the women. They sat in Princess Nadja's palace home surrounded by sleeping babies and trays of decadent chocolate. Her high-backed chair practically swallowed her in comfort. "Mirek and I have a special bond."

Nadja and Olek had a relaxing home filled with life—from the abundance of plants, to the center water fountain in the front hall, to the walls of giant fish tanks.

"What do you mean special?" Princess Morrigan asked. She cradled her son in her lap. The baby already showed signs of being strong-willed. He had his mother's dark hair and his father's brown eyes. Morrigan lightly stroked his hair, causing the thin strands to stand up in a strip of hair down the center of his head.

"We feel each other," Riona said. "I don't know how it happened, but I can sometimes feel him so much that his mind becomes clear to me."

"And he calls you from across the castle?" Nadja asked. Her son lay in a bassinet. The boy was a tiny little thing, but with the way he ate he'd soon catch up to the others.

Riona nodded. "Yes."

"All the Draig couples have that," Olena said, bouncing her red-headed son to keep him from fussing too loud. Riona couldn't help but smile when she thought of the woman who'd drunk whiskey with her on the Galaxy Brides ship and spoke of marriage like it was something to mock. Oh, how time had changed that woman's tune. Olena was completely smitten with her Prince Yusef.

"They do?" Riona asked in surprise. She looked at Aeron, who nodded in confirmation. Baby Lantos snuggled next to Clara's and Kendall's newborn sons on a blanket. The three boys were constantly in each other's company when they were at the fortress home.

"Bron uses it to make food requests," Aeron drawled. "I finally managed to block him, after he kept making me visualize my hands stirring a giant pot of stew."

"That's what you get for trying to cook," Kendall said. "Alek never visualizes me using a food simulator."

The women laughed.

"Ask the queen. She will tell you all about it. I'm pretty sure she gave all of us *the lecture*." Pia made a face even though her tone was ominous. "At least she did to us princesses."

In the room full of baby boys, there was only one girl—Zoran and Pia's daughter. It was kind of perfect that a girl was born to the largest, most fierce of all the princes. Pia confessed that she'd already called off three of her husband's soldiers who had been ordered to act as the baby's bodyguard. Though Riona could see why Zoran would worry as a father. Already the baby showed a strong favor to her mother's stellar looks. But in some ways Riona felt bad for the girl child. She would be raised around boys and she was already set to be married to a Var prince. It was part of the peace agreement with the cat-shifters.

"No," Aeron said, "I'm pretty sure I got it from the queen too, when we came here to warn them about the Tyoe."

"Ah, I missed out on that," Clara said. "What did she say?"

"That, insert husband's name, had put every chance at happiness in, insert wife's name," Morrigan stated regally, mimicking the queen's voice.

"Oh, and he gave his life to you," Pia added. She looked at Olena.

"Um," Olena bit her lip thoughtfully. "Fighting

always makes warriors happy, for it's something they know how to do?"

Laughter again rang throughout the home. Pia and Morrigan grabbed their sides and Nadja struggled to breathe.

"I'm pretty sure that's the wrong lecture," Pia stated.

"Huh." Olena shrugged. "Honestly, I kind of daydreamed through some of her lecturing. Oh, I believe it was something about how married men can't have sex with other women because of the whole crystal breaking and…I think around that time they brought in a tray of food and I just stopped listening."

"She said they share their life with you," Nadja inserted softly. "I think it's terribly romantic."

"Yes, well done, ladies," Morrigan nodded regally before continuing on with her impersonation, "By giving you his life, he shortened his and extended yours so your fates could remain together. If you were to choose to leave him, he would be alone for the rest of his days."

Though they were joking around, Riona found herself listening intently.

"I do not sound like that," Queen Mede scolded from the doorway.

Morrigan gasped, looking properly horrified

before laughing. "I was trying to give your lecture the right tone."

"I don't lecture," the queen stated. She began making the rounds to each child, kissing their heads. "But if I did lecture, you ladies deserved it and much more. We have never had a more stubborn batch of brides."

Clara, Kendall, Aeron and Riona all laughed at the princesses.

"I was talking about you ladies as well," Mede said. It was the princesses' turn to laugh.

"So what does this life force exchange have to do with my feeling Mirek?" Riona could feel her husband now, even though he was out of the room.

"Oh, well you didn't tell her the best part," the queen said, kissing another head. "When you are bonded completely, you will be able to hear his thoughts in your head. You'll sense his troubles. You'll hear him call to you from across the palace. You'll know every moment he wants you, when he's sick, when he's hiding something from you in an effort to protect you."

"And he'll be able to place an order for dinner," Aeron added.

"What's this about dinner?" Bron asked, leading the husbands into the room. "I'm suddenly very hungry for stew."

Riona smiled and instantly stood to greet

Mirek. She went to him and slid into his arms to kiss him.

"Not stew," Alek said. "Great-grandfather's Qurilixian rum. The ladies can finally drink it and this seems like the perfect celebration to break open the old bottle."

"Save me a glass. I have to attend the ceremony," the queen said as she left.

"I missed you," Riona whispered to Mirek.

"Not I," he answered. "For I carry you inside me always."

Riona hit his arm. "You're lucky that's a sweet answer."

She turned to witness the happy couples and their children.

"I had to tease Sven about his loincloth," Vlad was saying to Clara. "You should have seen it. Arianwen, uh, decorated it for him."

"Ri, I know you're up for a drink," Alek said. "If this is as strong as I think it is, it's possible we'll be causing some serious mischief down at the festival later. Kendall and Mirek might have to bail us out of trouble."

Riona laughed. "Sorry, brother, none for me."

"Ah." Alek pretended to be hurt. "You have to try it. We've waited a long time to open this bottle."

"She has plans tonight," Mirek stated, holding her closer.

"Actually, now that we're all here, I wanted to say something," Riona announced. When their eyes turned to her, she had a moment of hesitation at the direct attention. Mirek touched her arm and the hesitation went away. "After what Aeron and I went through as children, I never thought I'd want to call a place home. I'm glad I was wrong. This planet has given me a family. I love you all."

"Aw." Nadja began to tear up.

The group returned her sentiment, the women more openly than their warrior husbands, who offered their blessings and reaffirmed her standing as their kin.

"And—" Riona turned to Mirek as the talking died down once more, "—I'm very happy to announce that our family will soon be complete." She took her husband's hand and placed it on her stomach. Softly, she said, "Aeron and I checked the medical booth earlier to confirm my suspicions."

Mirek's eyes rounded. With a hearty laugh, he lifted her up off the ground and spun her around the room. Congratulations exploded around them, so loud it woke the babies who began to cry. Mirek placed his wife on the floor. As he moved in to kiss her, he whispered, "You have given me so much, wife. How can I ever begin to repay you?"

She pulled back and let a mischievous smile curl her lip. "You did remember to pack that loincloth, right?" He nodded. "Good. Now grab a tray of the chocolate and take me to our tent. I want to celebrate properly."

Mirek nearly tripped over himself to obey and soon he'd swept his wife in his arms, dumped chocolate on her lap, and was running out of the palace amidst the amazed laughter of their family.

The End

The series continues with The Dragon's Queen.

THE SERIES CONTINUES…

The books continue!

Dragon Lords 9: The Dragon's Queen

Want to see how King Attor's sons turn out, despite their father's teachings?

Lords of the Var®: The Savage King

Read all the Dragon Lords and Var books? Yay, you, keep going!

Space Lords 1: His Frost Maiden

THE DRAGON'S QUEEN

BY MICHELLE M. PILLOW

Dragon Lords Series

Bestselling Shape-shifter Romance

Mede of the Draig knows three things for a fact: As the only female dragon-shifter of her people, she is special. She can kick the backside of any man. And she absolutely doesn't want to marry.

Mede has spent a lifetime trying to prove herself as strong as any male warrior. Unfortunately, being the special, rare creature she is, she's been claimed as the future bride to nearly three dozen Draig—each one confident that when they come for her hand in marriage fate will choose them. When the men aren't bragging about how they're going to marry her, they're acting like she's a delicate rare flower in need of their protection.

She is far from a shrinking solarflower.

Prince Llyr of the Draig knows four things for a fact: He is the future king of the dragon-shifters. He must act honorably in all ways. He absolutely, positively is meant to marry Lady Mede. And she dead set against marriage.

Llyr's fate rests in the hands of a woman determined not to have any man. With a new threat emerging amongst their cat-shifting neighbors, a threat whose eyes are focused firmly on Mede, time may be running out. It is up to him to convince her to be his dragon queen.

The Dragon's Queen Extended Excerpt

Mede's lungs expanded with the effort of a hard run. Morning crept over the horizon, brightening the light of night. In one hand she gripped Rolant's knife, and in the other, her prize. For a moment, she felt perfection in the burn of her legs, the pant of her breath, the rhythm of her feet. When she jumped over forest debris, she flew.

The exercise felt wonderful, but not nearly as wonderful as the sounds of cheers coming from the border. They had lit a fire to guide her back and she ran toward it. As she neared the group of dragons she leapt over the border. Lifting her hand, she yelled, "Dragons!"

"Dragons!" the men yelled, celebrating her victorious run.

Mede turned the hilt of the knife toward Rolant to return the blade. He took it. Instantly, his smile faded as he saw the blood. His eyes roamed her as she let the dragon-shift fade from her body. Before he could ask her about it, she proudly lifted her fist balled around the fur. "Victory!"

"Victory!" the men yelled, clearly well into their cups. While she had her adventure, they'd partied.

"Our lady found the still," Arthur said, with a laugh as he sniffed the liquor fumes on her. The man had a crook to his nose from having been punched a few too many times. When he drank, he liked to brawl.

"How is the mangy cat?" Cynan asked.

"Owain remembers you fondly," Mede answered, grinning. A round of shouts and laughter cut off the conversation. After it finally died down, she held out her hand. "My prize."

A few of the men looked down at her

outstretched hand, then a couple more. Their laughter died as they took in her achievement.

"That doesn't look like..." Saben gave her a questioning look.

Dylan reached to pinch a bit of the fur. "It's blond."

"Mede?" Rolant inquired, clearly wishing she'd explain. "Didn't you find the still?"

"Yes, but I wanted a harder target," she said. "Besides, the still farmer was already missing a lot of tufts. I felt sorry for him."

Rolant lifted the blade, showing the blood to the others. "Who did you fight?"

Mede thought of the stranger. There was no reason to tell them what had happened. They didn't need to know the cat-shifter had kissed her. That would be her secret.

"We didn't exchange names." She gave a little shrug of dismissal.

"Test it, so none my challenge her claim," Rolant said. There was a lot of fumbling as they searched for a particular satchel that held the genetic testing fluid. As the others were distracted, Rolant pulled her aside. "I sent you to the still farmer. What were you thinking? The only blond Var I have seen belong to the elite palace guard. That or the prince. How did you get it? Why is there blood on—?"

"It's good!" Dylan yelled, lifting a small vial to pour testing liquid onto the ground. When the cat-shifter fur combined with the chemicals it turned the test liquid a pale blue color. "It's Var."

"Not now, Rolant," Mede said. "I need a drink."

A bottle was instantly shoved in her direction. She drank deeply of the liquor. It stung her throat and warmed her belly.

"Tell us of the run," Cynan said.

"What's this?" a male voice boomed over the encampment.

Mede was relieved for it saved her from having to tell that particular fireside story.

"Do you have permission to be on my land?" the stranger continued.

Mede lowered the bottle and wiped her mouth on her sleeve. She didn't recognize the voice. Several of the men blocked her view. Since they were camped on palace land with Prince Rolant she wasn't too concerned by the claim.

"Brother!" Rolant acknowledged. "You've returned. I thought you were hunting yorkins."

"Gildas was injured. Nothing serious, but we decided to bring him home so he could have the proper medical attention," Prince Llyr answered.

Mede changed her mind. She didn't like the interruption. This was her victory morning. She didn't want to meet a new male Draig, and certainly not the heir prince. The prince was not married and had already told Rolant he wanted to meet her.

"Hand me a drink," Llyr said. "Whose victory are we celebrating?"

Like grasses being blown aside by a stout wind, the men parted to let Llyr see her. She stiffened and automatically lifted her jaw. "Mine."

"You?" Llyr repeated in disbelief. He looked at Rolant for confirmation. "And she passed?"

"And we saw her fly," Saben inserted.

"That was you who flew," Arthur said.

"Oh, right." Saben nodded. He lifted his cup and announced. "And I flew!"

"How is Owain?" Llyr asked.

"In need of a bath," Mede said.

"She brought back blond fur," Rolant stated.

"Blond...?" Llyr handed the bottle he held to his brother and stepped forward to look at her.

Mede was glad she smelled like a liquor still and sweat. And she probably looked like a wild beast after her run. She forced herself not to look at his chest to see his crystal. Looking at his face was worse.

In many ways he reminded her of Rolant, only his eyes were a brighter green—so bright they penetrated her, taking her in as if he could see all her secrets. Mede didn't like to feel exposed. His light brown hair hung to his chin whereas Rolant's was much longer. She thought of the kiss the Var had stolen from her. She had not been expecting it and really had felt nothing but surprise when it happened, but the memory caused her eyes to dart down to Llyr's mouth.

"Finally we meet, Lady Medellyn," he said.

Mede forced her eyes away from his firm lips. She swallowed nervously. "I am called Mede. And I am not a lady. Today I am a Dead Dragon."

At the words the inebriated men cheered. "Dead Dragons!"

Llyr chuckled. More to himself than to her, he said, "I can see the liquor has not gone to waste here."

"If you'll excuse me, prince, I want my scar." She made a move to leave his presence, still refusing to look down. The idea that a prince would be her mate terrified her. She'd never wanted this meeting.

"Wait," Llyr said, being so bold as to grab her arm. "I should like to congratulate you on a good run."

Mede arched a brow. The more she found herself mesmerized by his eyes, the more stubborn her demeanor became. When he didn't speak, she said, "Well?"

"Congratulations on a good run," he answered softly.

"Thank you, prince," she answered dutifully before moving to skirt past him. The men had started to sing a bawdy song as they linked arms and began a noisy, drunken chain through the campsite. The prancing took them away from where she stood. She wished they'd circle back.

Llyr grabbed her arm again. "Did you really take the fur from a member of the royal court?"

At the time she hadn't been nervous, but now, the way both Llyr and Rolant mentioned the fur color, made her suddenly a little sick to her stomach. Nerves bunched in her chest and she nodded once. "I suppose I did though at the time I didn't ask for his name."

"What did he look like?"

"A cat," she answered, being difficult on purpose. His fingers lingered on her arm, the touch somehow intimate. Finally she got the nerve to look down. At first, she thought she might have seen a soft glow in the stone. Only on the festival night would it light to full power. She stiffened, until she realized that it must have been firelight reflection. He was not her mate. A sigh of relief whispered past her lips…followed by a sense of disappointment. The disappointment confused her and made her want to run away like a coward.

"Have you mated?" Llyr asked, eyeing her neck.

Always to that.

She lowered her eyes over her lashes. "I have no interest in marriage. I would like my scar though." She tried to pull her arm.

He tightened his grip. "So it is true. You broke your own crystal. Why?"

Mede grimaced, remembering that day long ago. Her mother had wept openly for months over it. "So did you." She reached for his chest, pinching the crystal from where it laid against him and gave it a little toss. It bounced against him. An almost microscopic thin crack marred the inside of the stone.

"An accident when I was a boy trick riding ceffyls," Llyr said.

"My father is a ceffyl breeder. You should not be trick riding them," she lectured. "They are in delicate supply and not for games."

"I was a boy," he stated, enunciating the words. His attitude infuriated her.

"No excuse," she answered just as arrogantly.

"I broke my arm, if that helps."

"It's a start." She again tried to pull her arm free from his grasp.

The singing had reached the forest and the men disappeared behind a colossal tree. Somehow being alone with him made her nervous.

"Unhand me, prince," she said at last. "I earned my place here."

Llyr looked at her arm in surprise, as if he didn't know he held her. Instantly his fingers released her. "Tell me first, why did you crush your crystal?"

"What? I love me. I married myself." She wasn't sure why she was being obstinate or sarcastic. All she knew is that her arm tingled where he touched her. She glanced at his stone. It didn't glow. Still, the urge to run from him was great. Her muscles felt weak. Surely her body shook from the long night of exercise, nothing else. Her mind felt fuzzy because she was tired. It had nothing to do with his smell or those eyes. Those damned green eyes.

"Somehow I don't think you're truly that narcissistic, my lady."

"Very well. If you must know, it is because I make my own fate." Mede gave a little hop past him and went to join the dancing men. Saben and Cynan broke the chain to let her in. As they pulled her away from the prince, she was glad for the escape. Something about the man drew her in and frustrated the netherworld out of her. She was pretty sure it was his eyes. No man should ever possess eyes like that.

To find out more about Michelle's books visit www.MichellePillow.com

ABOUT MICHELLE M. PILLOW

New York Times* & *USA TODAY
Bestselling Author

Michelle loves to travel and try new things, whether it's a paranormal investigation of an old Vaudeville Theatre or climbing Mayan temples in Belize. She believes life is an adventure fueled by copious amounts of coffee.

Newly relocated to the American South, Michelle is involved in various film and documentary projects with her talented director husband. She is mom to a fantastic artist. And she's managed by a dog and cat who make sure she's meeting her deadlines.

For the most part she can be found wearing pajama pants and working in her office. There may or may not be dancing. It's all part of the creative process.

Come say hello! Michelle loves talking with readers on social media!

www.MichellePillow.com

facebook.com/AuthorMichellePillow
twitter.com/michellepillow
instagram.com/michellempillow
bookbub.com/authors/michelle-m-pillow
goodreads.com/Michelle_Pillow
amazon.com/author/michellepillow
youtube.com/michellepillow
pinterest.com/michellepillow

COMPLIMENTARY EXCERPTS

TRY BEFORE YOU BUY!

REBELLIOUS PRINCE

BY MICHELLE M. PILLOW

Captured by a Dragon-Shifter

A Modern Day Dragon Lords Story

A Qurilixen World Novel

Cat-shifter Prince Rafe knows that technically he's supposed to be going to Earth to find a bride, but he doesn't see the need to rush things. While his dragon-shifter neighbors appear all too eager to claim their mates and settle down, he's all for putting that final moment off and enjoying his little trips through the portal. Yeah, yeah, eventually he'll have to marry and set a good example for his people because on his planet females are rare and they need to have children and blah blah blah. But honestly, cat-shifters are known to embrace their feral side and it would take a very impressive female to tame his.

Then he sees Jenna Kearney and all bets are off.

To find out more about Michelle's books visit www.MichellePillow.com

HIS METAL MAIDEN

BY MICHELLE M. PILLOW

A Space Lords Novel

Dragon-shifter Lochlann left home to avoid a war he didn't believe in. Now as Captain of The Conqueror, in charge of a misfit crew, all he wants is to return without the label of coward. He's been offered one chance at redemption: Find Margot, a noblewoman's missing sister. The only problem is, the woman disappeared years ago, and his closest lead is a stunningly beautiful look-a-like droid crafted in her image. Alexis is programed to be everything he could ever desire, but getting her to reveal her secrets proves to be a true challenge for this alpha male.

Being a base model pleasure droid isn't as glamorous as it sounds. Alexis can't remember a time when she wasn't the property of others. Multiple surgeries, and endless tests, have amounted to a life not worth living. When a pirate crew visits her facility, she sneaks onto their ship. Desperate not to be returned to her owners, she strikes a deal with the alluring captain. Pretend to be Margot in exchange for freedom.

CHAPTER ONE EXCERPT

The Conqueror, Deep Space

"Solar balls and black holes!" Rick ran into the common area of the ship. Breathing hard, he panted, "Alarm. Alarm. Cockpit. Alarm."

Captain Lochlann turned his halfhearted attention toward the pilot. Many of Rick's outbursts were just fits of boredom, or signs of mischief, or, worse, bored mischief that would land them in some intergalactic quagmire. Ever since the pilot had brought a Lintianese curse down on their heads, Lochlann had lost patience for the man's antics.

Lochlann's situation was complicated enough without having his future love life doomed before it began. According to his dragon-shifter people's custom, in order to marry he needed to be on his home planet on their one night of darkness to participate in the breeding ceremony. That wouldn't be such a big deal, except for the fact he was banned from returning to his home planet. Not only couldn't he marry in accordance with his people's beliefs, the chance of finding a woman at all was cursed to fail thanks to Rick's big mouth. Mating was hard enough for dragons. They weren't like other alien cultures. When they married, it was for life. One woman. One wife. One chance at happiness.

"What did you do now, Rick? Asteroids, mine fields, Federation vessels, or ex-girlfriend?" Lochlann drawled, unconcerned. Being in charge of space pirates wasn't something he'd asked for. It just happened. Life was unexpected that way.

Though, to be fair, they weren't *true* space pirates. More like borderline mini-pirates. They didn't follow all the galaxy's laws, but then they didn't attack innocent spaceships and intentionally harm people. They were adventurers—planet-less adventurers—joined together by brotherhood, wanderlust, and a shared need to survive.

"Actually, don't answer. Just fix it." Without indulging whatever Rick was going on about, Lochlann turned back to the game grid before him. Jackson had acquired the new board for Frendle's Chips on their last fuel stop. Metal discs hovered above the grid. Random currents of electricity ran between them in short bursts. The goal was to first sweep the discs out of the grid without getting shocked. Then you had to toss the discs back into place without letting them touch the electricity. Otherwise your disc would turn into particles. The game was popular with serious gamblers, but they were having a hell of a time mastering it.

"There has to be an easier way to win money. Want me to fix it so you never lose?" Viktor was their mechanic and could pretty much rig anything.

"Some of us don't need to cheat to win," Lucien said, mostly to be contrary to his brother. Slender and pale with red-green and red-brown eyes, Viktor and Lucien took after their Dere heritage more than their human side. Irrelevant arguments were pretty much the only way they communicated with each other.

"Cockpit alarm," Rick repeated louder from the doorway when no one gave him the reaction he was looking for. They continued to ignore him.

"No, you're not rigging my board," Jackson asserted. Out of all the current crewmen, he'd been with Lochlann the longest. The man had a secretive military background and, up until very recently, had spent most of his time in the ship's VR room training with his security officer counterpart, Dev. However, since Dev fell in love with Violette Stephens, he didn't have much time for training anymore. Now Jackson was on some strange, almost lonely quest to master every challenge that crossed his path.

Violette's half-sister was also on board. They'd rescued Josselyn Craven from an ice prison, and she'd married the ship's empath, Evan Cormier. Violette and Josselyn weren't the best of friends, and like Viktor and Lucien they bickered if they were left in each other's company for too long. For that reason, he'd encourage their husbands to keep them out of the common area and in their quarters during longer trips.

Maybe arguing was a sibling thing. Lochlann had no idea. He didn't have brothers or sisters.

"We need to do something to earn space credits," Viktor stated. "Our last treasure hunt was a bust, and there is no way I'm ever going back to that abandoned icehole called Florencia's Fifth Moon to search for a third time. My balls still have frostbite."

"That's not frostbite. You have to have balls before they can..." Lucien tried to reach over the active game grid to swipe a disc. Electricity zapped his finger, and he jumped back. Shaking his injured hand, he finished weakly, "be bitten."

"Zenni District," Rick stated, the words softer than before.

That got their attention. All eyes turned toward him.

"Your sex life does not constitute an emergency. We don't have the space credits to afford a pleasure droid," Lochlann denied the unspoken request. He knew being a single man forced to see two happy couples every day in the close confines of the ship wasn't easy. Sacred cats, he was lonely too. He'd love to buy a pleasure droid to fake companionship on desolate nights. "And we're not burning fuel to go to the Zenni District so that you can walk around and gaze longingly into canister pods in a storage facility."

"We have to go. There's an alarm," Rick insisted.

"What do you keep saying about an alarm?" Jackson frowned. "I have received no security notices."

"Captain Jarek must have set it before he went home. The computers are running a continuous scan for, um, something important," Rick explained ineloquently. "I think in honor of our former captain, we should go to the Zenni District to see about the match the alarm has found."

A zapping noise drew Lochlann's attention back to the game.

Lucien sucked on an injured knuckle and glared at the grid. "You stupid…*game*."

Lochlann missed his captain predecessor. Jarek had been his friend since they were boys shifting and running in the woods of their home planet. They'd left Quirlixen because they saw no other choice. Lochlann was a Draig dragon-shifter and Jarek was a Var cat-shifting prince. Their people had been at war in some age-old feud that no one understood. The fighting was so ingrained that even during times of peace they still had petty skirmishes. It wasn't like they fought over territory, or social injustice. They just fought because both sides didn't seem to like the other.

Lochlann hadn't wanted to kill anyone. Prince Jarek felt the same. So they left for offworld adventures. Jarek had captained the crew since he was a prince and it was his ship, and Lochlann had been his second in command. Everything had been so new and shiny back then.

But that was years ago. The Draig-Var war had ended, supposedly for good with the death of Jarek's father. Lochlann had his doubts. Peace never seemed to last.

For him, adventures had turned into a way of life, life turned into normal, and now he was no longer Lochlann of the Draig, dragon-shifter exploring space who had a home planet. No, now he was Captain Lochlann of *The Conqueror*, newly in charge of a misfit crew and a traitor on his homeworld for refusing to kill cat-shifters.

Jarek had promoted him before moving home

to the Var palace with his wife and infant son. The prince's brothers welcomed him with open arms as if he'd never left. The Draig were not as understanding with Lochlann.

A battle had taken Lochlann's father. Grief killed his mother. He had no siblings. As was the dragon way, others raised him until he was old enough to train for war. He never went hungry, never was without a place to sleep, and had usually been treated kindly, but he was passed from home to home. He'd been a community responsibility.

His youthful decision not to fight didn't go over too well with his people. All he wanted was to remove the label of traitor from his name. He had to restore his honor before he could return home, and the dragon-shifter nobles had given him a way to do just that.

It should have been simple. He had to find one lost human and bring her back to her noblewoman sister. How hard would it be to track one girl? It's not like this Margot was some kind of master criminal. She was a girl from a space fuel dock.

Then why in all the black hole, cursed port, bloody novas could he not complete that one task to find the blasted Margot?

He couldn't even find a trail to follow.

"It's the responsible thing to do," Rick insisted, drawing Lochlann's attention back.

"Is this alarm a sales notification?" Lochlann drawled wryly.

"I don't think Jarek's wife would appreciate his shopping for a pleasure droid," Jackson added.

Lochlann knew for a fact Jarek would never shop for such a thing. He was madly in love with his wife.

"The fact that the pleasure droid manufacturer is located there is not why we're going," Rick said, "but there was an alarm set to go off to let Jarek know, and we need to—"

"I'm thinking Rick may have a point," Viktor interrupted. "And I am in no way basing my opinion on the encoded airwaves Lucien decrypted of the new pleasure droid model advertisements."

"I *am* completely basing my vote on that," Lucien said. "I say Zenni District."

"This is not up for a vote," Lochlann stated. "We're low on space credits, and fuel reserves. It's my job to make sure we make responsible decisions and don't end up floating in the deep black hoping someone reputable rescues our sorry asses."

"What is the alarm for specifically?" Jackson asked.

"Something called a mar-got," Rick said with a shrug.

Lochlann stiffened. "Did you say Margot?"

"What's a Margot?" Jackson asked.

"A girl," Lochlann whispered. It couldn't be. His chest tightened, and he found it hard to breathe.

He missed home. He wanted to see the red dirt and green-tinted skies, to shift into dragon form and run through the shadowed marshes near the borderlands. Instead, he was condemned to the high skies, sailing the deep black looking for a woman who might never be found.

Until now.

Had he finally found Margot?

PLEASE LEAVE A REVIEW

THANK YOU FOR READING!

Please take a moment to share your thoughts by leaving a review.

Be sure to check out Michelle's other titles at

www.michellepillow.com

Printed in Great Britain
by Amazon